The Talisman Series

The Search For Synergy

By

Brett Salter

The Search For Synergy

Copyright © 2017 Brett Salter

All rights reserved.

ISBN-10:1542914841

ISBN-13:978-1542914840

Dedication

To my loves: Allison (my soulmate), Jackson (J.G), and Quinn (Trouble).

To my family and friends for all their love and support over the years.

To Monica Erwin who breathed fire into this project.

Special thanks to Bonnie DeMoss for her editing expertise

The Search For Synergy

Check out all of *The Talisman Series* by Brett Salter

"The Search For Synergy" (*The Talisman Series* Book #1

"Riders of Fire and Ice" (*The Talisman Series* Book #2)

"Windy City Ruins" (*The Talisman Series* Book #3)

"The Battle For Verdana" (*The Talisman Series* Book #4)

The Search For Synergy

The Search For Synergy

"Some people spend their lives in search for answers in someone else's eyes. Some people fear they're gonna fade away so they live just to remind." — Jason Cruz

Chapter One

School….yuck! School was not always yuck. Until recently, Rome had liked school. But today seemed unbearably slow. He wasn't sure what had changed. It could be the anticipation of summer, but he doubted that. He had an unnerving fear that the something that had changed was him. He felt uneasy just sitting still. He needed to move; to physically release the burning need for action. Was this one of the changes Coach had described in that "special" Health Class he had last semester? If so, he seemed to be the only one going through it. Rome looked around the class. Most of the kids were paying attention to the teacher. Those who weren't looked entangled in a waking sleep: eyes opened, brains closed.

He started to fidget. "Control," he thought. "Keep it under control." His go-to mantra that had worked for years when he was experiencing his bouts of twitching was less and less effective these days.

What was happening to him couldn't be normal, could it? If it wasn't, what could he do? What he needed was someone to talk to about this. None of his friends were close enough for that. He needed to find some way to release this energy, and it had to be tonight. He couldn't wait any longer. Now he just had to figure out what to do. It was at that precise moment that an idea formulated in his head. It was an idea that seemed to mirror the burning inside. Tonight! He would rectify this tonight.

When the day finally ended, Rome rushed home. He called greetings to his mother and flew up the stairs to his bedroom. Rome began a systematic rummaging of the room. He knew what he was looking for, but couldn't remember where he had hidden the contraband fireworks from last 4th of July. After several, stress-filled minutes of searching, Rome found the package of Black Cat firecrackers under several pairs of blue and black socks in his bottom drawer. What would the evening hold? What would he feel like when he was done? What was wrong with him?

"Sometimes I have just got to add a touch of wicked excitement to my humdrum existence," Rome said to himself. He didn't always talk to himself, but lately he had been thinking more and speaking less. Realizing that nobody can hear what is in your head is a marvelous thing about growing up. All the inane, rambling thoughts of a thirteen-year old who is bored out of his wits living in a small town in Georgia may sound a bit fanciful or maybe completely fanatical. Now, all he had to do was wait for dinner.

After dinner, Rome made up an excuse about getting help with homework, and he left the house promising to be home by nine o' clock. He hated deceiving his mother, but this little white lie could not possibly hurt anyone. Tomorrow he would ask Clay to cover for him, if the question ever arose.

"I mean, it's not like I'm going to blow up the whole neighborhood," he reminded himself. Without a second thought, he slipped around to the back of the house, away from prying eyes. Immediately, he was struck by a question. Was he trying to bolster his courage to strike, or was he trying to convince himself that there was a valid reason for this act of lunacy? He intended to light up the night with some ear-blasting, neighborhood-shaking, friendly fire. Of course, intent rarely ever equates to outcome.

This was it; his first, but probably not his last act of rebellion. He knew that consequences would be swift and excruciating if he got caught. He did not care. He just had to DO something. There was an inexplicable need to push the limits of his parents' control, yet he did not know why. This insane need to commit an act of insurgence felt right. This uncontrollable feeling had begun building up inside of his head weeks ago, and no amount of fidgeting or twitching could release the tension. The need to rebel kept growing like a flower blooming. No, that comparison was too sweet to describe the way he felt. The feeling was more like a snake shedding its skin. He felt all trapped in a life too small and needed to break out. Yeah, that was more like it! He had an insatiable need to be free. Free of what? Not a clue.

At first, he tried to be cool with his pyrotechnics. He struck the match against the sole of his left Puma just like all the action heroes did. He quickly realized this was not going to work. Matches needed something abrasive to ignite the sulfur, not rubber. He decided to try it against something with a little more grit. The pavement would provide the perfect amount of both resistance and friction to light the match.

Of course, after two or three tries, the match snapped in half, and Rome briefly thought about giving up on his tour de force. "Am I so bored that even a burned finger is worth it?" He paused in mid-thought. "Most definitely, yes," he concluded.

Abruptly, he noticed something out of the corner of his eye. The match head seemed to be moving in his fingers. It appeared to be changing into individual pixels right before his eyes. The pixels moved like a television that had lost its signal. They bounced back and forth excitedly, yet remained contained on the bulbous red tip of the match. He shook his head and blinked his eyes trying to right his vision, but the pixels still jumped around the match head.

"What in the world is that all about?" Rome asked himself as he brought the match closer to his face for a more intense inspection. "Am I hallucinating?" he thought. He squinted one more time to try to bring his vision back in line, when he felt his eyes tearing up with warmth. In a split second, that warmth turned to heat. Then, it turned into extreme heat. Rome felt the skin on his cheeks heating up, and he smelled hair burning.

His head was on fire! No! Not his head! His eyes were on fire!

He cupped his hands over both of his eyes and threw himself to the ground. His mind raced. He reached out and found a small watering can his mother kept around to water her flowering plants in the nearby gardens. In a panic, he began fervently splashing handfuls of water into his eyes. As the burn intensified, he frantically pelted his face with any liquid he could find in a desperate attempt to put out the fire.

The heat ended as suddenly as it came. Rome stopped thrashing around. He pulled his hands away from his eyes and stared into the puddle he had created on the ground. He half expected his eyes to be burned to a crisp. Miraculously, they were unharmed. He blinked three or four times and realized his vision was okay. He feverishly patted down his cheeks and traced the curves of his face but everything seemed to be intact. That's when he had a crazy realization.

"I am not hurt!" he exclaimed. "I am not burned or anything! There is no pain!" Try as he could, he didn't remember feeling any pain at all. What about his hair? He had surely smelled burning hair if only for a brief second. He again, glanced down at his reflection in the water. "My hair is perfectly fine!" he cried out.

Rome stood up to better assess what had just happened. He touched his clothes. All okay. His mom would be happy about that. He looked around the area. Everything seemed normal. Then, he noticed the half matchstick he had been holding when the event happened. It was there on the ground about five feet behind him, and the head was obsidian black. In fact, the whole match was burnt to a crisp.

Suddenly, the heat started again. This time it wasn't on his face. It was at his back. He whirled around and could not believe his eyes. A large-standing crape myrtle belonging to his neighbor Mrs. Baskins was engulfed in red-orange flames shooting up to as high as the streetlight. Self-preservation took hold, and Rome ducked into a darkened area of his yard. He stood back a good twenty feet from the burning tree, but could still feel the licks of heat pouring off of it.

"Oh, horse-apples," he muttered louder than he meant to. "I am in some serious trouble." And with that, he ran as fast as he could around the house and into his living room. "Mom!" he shouted. "Mrs. Baskins' yard....there's a tree....uh....Mom, call the fire station now!" He sounded panicked. Rome was never panicked. He was usually cool, collected, and very deliberate with his thoughts and actions. Something was different this time. Something strange had happened to him out there that he could not explain. He was freaked out!

Within minutes, he heard the fire engine wail. He stood by the front window watching the firefighters douse what was left of the tree with fire retardant chemicals. Luckily, the fire had not spilled onto the neighbor's yard. That was because Mrs. Baskins was a meticulous gardener and made sure her grass was healthy, green, and watered all year round. It was something for which Rome would forever be in her debt. But the myrtle had been vibrant and healthy also. How had something so alive been enflamed so quickly by a tiny match?

Rome reached into his pocket and felt for the fireworks. They were still there, unused. They could not have been the reason for the combustion. Then, he remembered the panic and crazy heat he had felt in his eyes. He couldn't remember any pain though. That wasn't the strangest part to him. He began to believe that maybe HE had started that inferno. Maybe HE had burned through the match and caught the tree on fire. Something strange had happened to him out there for sure. What he wanted to know now was where did the fire come from? His head swam. There was no doubt. His mind was fanatical, not fanciful. And the ever-present urge to shed his skin still pulled at him.

It had been such a long day at school, and it was shaping up to be an even longer night. The days had a tendency to drag on where he lived, and soon he would find how unbelievably exciting those days could be.

Chapter Two

The next day, Rome trudged along the Dampier Middle School hallways like a member of the undead. They roamed like herd of cows meandering between classes, with the inexperienced sixth-graders just as lost today as they had been on day one of the school year. Rome chuckled to himself thinking about how lost he had been two years prior when he was a lowly sixth-grader. He had really come into his own here at Dampier Middle School though. He enjoyed being a "Fighting Husky" (the school's mascot). He got along with all the cliques and didn't really have any enemies to speak of. Rome thought of middle school as the baby steps towards true peer segregation. Once kids got to high school, they could really dig into an affiliation of like-minded kids and start ostracizing the rest of their fellow students. At least here, there was still a small sense of camaraderie.

Rome felt optimistic on his way to lunch. This was his favorite time of day. He got to recharge his batteries and chow down on some grub. Thankfully, he also got to take a break from learning. And finally, he got to hang out with some friends and do what all scholarly and academically elite students do…..Play hackey sack!

Right after scarfing down their lunches, Rome and his buddies always went outside and got a hackey sack circle going. It was a great way to kill time and show off one's skills. Plus it was exercise and social bonding! Rome thought hackey sack should be an Olympic sport or at least on the Physical Education curriculum.

"Okay, spread it out guys," said one of Rome's cronies named Clay snacking on a beef jerky. Clay was a pretty big kid for his age assuming he was the same age as the rest of them. He played on the Junior Varsity football team and was definitely one of the cool kids. The rest of the circle included Samantha the tomboy, Flynn the soccer player, Will who lived in Rome's neighborhood, Aaron who played football with Clay, Josh A., and Josh B. (Josh B. went by "Bingham" since it was his last name and too many Josh's made for quite a confusing circle)

Sometimes other kids would come by and jump in, but for the most part, this was their core. On occasion Cecilia Parker would come by and watch. That was always when Rome tried his best to pull off some radical moves. He noticed her more than the rest of the girls at school.

They knocked out a few good rallies before Rome observed another kid named Julian watching from the brick wall leading into the cafeteria. Rome shrugged it off and continued the rest of his lunch break with his friends. When the bell finally rang for the next period, Rome again noticed that Julian was still watching. "What a weirdo," he thought to himself.

Apparently, it was quite obvious that Julian was watching Rome because Clay even came over and mentioned it to him. "Hey Rome, is that guy bothering you? Aaron and I could go talk to him for you if you want."

"No, that's okay," replied Rome. "Thank you though. I'm sure he's just taking note of my awesome tricks."

Clay laughed and bit into an apple. "Okay man. No worries. I've had my eye on that guy for a while. He's a little, ya know." Clay twirled his finger around his ear and crossed his eyes.

Now it was Rome's turn to laugh. Clay wasn't like most of the other football players. He was really down to Earth. Rome thought he must be an "old soul".

Rome, Samantha, and Josh A. headed to Math class, when Rome noticed his untied shoe. He was in front of the water fountain by the library, so he stepped to the fountain and leaned over to tie it while the others waited. As he bent down he noticed a small piece of graffiti etched into the lower, right corner of the water fountain. Rome could barely read it, but it looked like it said "Portal" in some very strange font. Rome looked closer. The graffiti shimmered.

"Hey, Sam! You guys go ahead without me. I'll catch up," he called to his friends. The word was definitely shining in the luminous lights. It was almost glowing. Rome wondered what type of polish or paint the originator of the marking had used to give it such a cool vibe. This thought floated in and out of his head as he tied his shoe.

Upon finishing his tie job, Rome stood up to follow his friends. However, he was shocked to see that Julian kid blocking his way. Julian was about the same height as Rome and had thick blonde hair that he pushed forward into a kind of faux-hawk. He had pastel, blue eyes that caught the attention of most of the seventh-grade girls. He was not an honor student by any means, but he did played on the soccer team and seemed to get along with most of the student body. His only real quirky feature was the fact he always had a die with him. It wasn't the kind of cheap plastic die one found in a Monopoly game. It was bulkier than most and made of wood. It looked like it was really old and dirty also. It was different than any die Rome had ever seen.

He hadn't thought anything of it the first time he saw it. Some kids had weird habits. For instance, Flynn carried a blue, lucky rabbit's foot to every home game. Aaron made some strange tongue-clicking noise every time someone let the hackey sack fall to the ground. Clay always wore the same shirt on Tuesdays. Julian, however, was pretty secretive about the die. One time he had been in the hackey sack circle with Rome's group and it fell out of his hand. Julian sprinted after the die, forsaking the game just so he could get to it before it rolled into the grass. That part ranked him right up there with lunatic status.

Julian and Rome stared at each other for several seconds before Julian spoke.

"Do you know the history of your Clan?" he asked Rome in a voice that was stern but not loud.

"What? My what? Clan? You've got me confused with someone else, Julian," Rome stuttered as he tried to push past the boy.

Julian extended his arm stopping Rome. "Never mind," Julian said almost reluctantly. "We can talk about that later. Right now you need to tell me how you did that thing with your eyes!"

"My eyes? What are you talking about, man?" Rome asked in a shaken voice. Suddenly, he felt threatened and a slow burn began in his stomach, like he had eaten too many jalapeno chips for lunch.

Julian grabbed Rome's arm and led him away from the water fountain towards the entrance to the library. In a much more hushed voice, Julian said, "I saw you after dinner outside your house. I saw what you did to that tree. I know who you are!" He looked around to make sure no one was watching them.

Rome brushed the accusation off. "I don't have any idea what you are talking about. You were not there."

"Oh yeah," Julian retorted. "How about when you said, "my hair is perfectly fine", and stared at yourself in the puddle like some kind of diva movie star?"

Rome became defensive. All semblance of friendliness disappeared. He felt the burning in his stomach grow stronger. This boy was a threat to him. He just knew it.

"I do not know what you think you know, but if you tell anyone I set that tree on fire, we are going to have a problem. I am not getting grounded for stealing my dad's fireworks and messing up Mrs. Baskin's yard. You and I have always been friendly towards each other." Rome's eyes burned.

Julian looked around as if not even listening to Rome. He had his die rolling around in his fingers. He looked back at Rome and gave a snarky smirk like he did not believe what Rome was saying. This kid had some nerve. Maybe Rome should take Clay up on his offer.

With a deep sigh and resignation Rome said, "Okay, you're right. I do not know what happened last night. I just know that I cannot afford to get in trouble. My parents are right on the edge of grounding me for life. How about we make a deal? You keep quiet and I will give you my Derek Jeter Rookie of the Year baseball card. It IS worth some money."

Julian stared for a moment and then burst out laughing. "You think I'm gonna rat you out for stealing your dad's fireworks?" He bent over at the hips to exaggerate how humorous this was to him, while cackling. "Dude, I'm not interested in holding you down. I'm interested in setting you free! Meet me at my place today after school. Let's say about....."

With that, Julian dropped his six-sided die onto the linoleum between the boys' feet. It rolled multiple times until it landed with a six facing up. Julian quickly looked up and smiled widely. "I'll see you at my place around 6:00" he said. He reached down and snatched the die off the ground, shuffled his book bag back onto his shoulder, and started off down the hallway.

Rome stood there by the library entrance silently for a minute or two. "Set me free?" he thought. "What is that kid talking about? There's no way I'm going over to his house tonight. This could be a trick. I go there, and the police show up?" Rome shook his head. "No way," he thought. Mrs. Baskins had already blamed the fire on some neighborhood punks who shoot off fireworks all the time. Was that kid serious? He definitely looked pretty serious.

"Maybe I'll go see what he has to say just to satisfy my curiosity". Rome was talking to himself again. "I mean, he's a cool kid, and the girls really like him. At worst, I'll spend the afternoon with a die-tossing weirdo engaged in a Dungeon and Dragons role-playing game or something. I guess I could always do my homework instead." Now that was a thought that Rome really despised.

Rome headed off to his next class. He figured he would keep the exchange with Julian to himself. There was no sense in letting his friends think he was some kind of freak that shot fire out of his eyes. I mean, nothing could be further from the truth, right?

Chapter Three

"What am I doing?" Rome asked himself as he navigated through the woods between his neighborhood and Julian's. He really didn't want to go talk to Julian, but he was interested in what the kid had to say. Why had Julian used the phrase "set him free"? What could he mean by that? Julian obviously knew something about what happened last night at Mrs. Baskin's house. However this played out, Rome was fairly sure he was going to be on the short end of the stick.

Suddenly, Rome's foot came down right in a shallow part of the creek that divided the neighborhoods. "Awww nuts!" he howled. Rome really, really, really disliked getting wet and now his foot was going to be soggy all night. Water was not his friend. Showers were okay because he disliked smelling bad even more, but Rome was just not a big fan of the water. He rarely went to swimming pools. He never visited the local waterpark, Camelot Adventureland. And he would always avoid the ocean at the beach. However, he did enjoy the wonderful, blazing sun on his face. When you're in water, you're wet. When you're wet, you're cold. Rome had preferred being warm over being cold as long as he could remember. Maybe this was HIS weird quirk?

While pondering the many pros and cons of the warm/cold debate in his mind, he realized he had made it all the way to Julian's house. Rome had been there a few times before. Pretty much everyone knew everyone in this town, and Rome remembered playing football in Julian's neighborhood when he was younger. The whole area was somewhat familiar to Rome. Maybe that is how Julian had seen him yesterday. It made sense. Kids went back and forth between neighborhoods all the time. Not to mention, the woods that separated all the neighborhoods were a really cool place to play in and get away from everything. Maybe Julian wasn't stalking him. Stalking him? Where did that come from?

Rome walked up to the house, but before he could start climbing the stairs, he heard Julian yell to him from the garage, which had silently opened without Rome even noticing. It even startled Rome to an extent, which seemed uncalled for.

"Hey, dude," Julian yelled. "I'm in here. I got something for you"

Cautiously, Rome approached the garage. He peered through the doors, trying to get up the courage to enter. He saw Julian straddling a bicycle and holding another one with his right arm. It looked like he was struggling a bit to balance both bikes, so Rome quickly grabbed the handlebars of the second bike to help out.

"We are actually gonna be leaving here and going somewhere else," Julian explained. "I was gonna have him come meet us here, but my dad's home, so we gotta go meet him." Rome was confused and more than a bit frightened, but he had made up his mind to see this through to the finish.

"Ooooo-kay," Rome fumbled. "Hey, I brought you that baseball card. You know? Wink-wink."

"Oh, perfect," Julian exclaimed. "I can stick it in the spokes and make my bike sound like a crazy, awesome, stunt bike!"

"You are being sarcastic, right?" asked Rome. The thought of Derek Jeter being bike fodder was scarier than anything that had happened yet.

Julian laughed. "Yeah! C'mon, dude. He's waiting for us. We're gonna set you free tonight!"

Julian hopped on his bike and rode off out the garage door. Rome waited for a few seconds, then jumped on the second bike and followed the strange kid down the street and onto the main road. They passed a few shopping centers and fast food places. They passed Flynn's house and Samantha's house too. Rome wondered where they were going. Why had he agreed to do this? Was it just his morbid curiosity? What was that old saying about curiosity and a cat?

Before Rome could muse on that subject any longer, he saw Julian swerve right into a small parking lot. Immediately, Rome knew where they were. It was the old library that had been around since Rome was a baby. He remembered going there on a field trip in third grade because the library at his elementary school was "limited" to say the least.

"Great," Rome thought. "He's probably bringing me to some nerdy book club or Magic: The

Gathering meeting. Now that die he carries around with him all the time makes sense."

Rome thought about pulling a quick U-turn, heading back to Julian's house, dropping off the bike, and putting this strange night behind him until something caught his eye. There was a peculiar symbol to the right of one of the main library window trim. As Rome and Julian walked to the front door, Rome stared at the unusual icon. Weirdly, he recognized the symbol. It was the same as the one from the water fountain by the library at school. Rome moved closer to get a better view of the sign. Sure enough, this marking said the same word, "Portal". At least, that's what Rome thought it said. It was quite difficult to read since it was fairly old and a little bit eroded. And not quite all there, if that made sense?

"Can you read that scribbling right there?" Rome asked Julian who had followed him to the window.

Julian looked at Rome with knowing eyes and a thin smirk. "You're starting to see them now," he said. "That's good! We need to remember everywhere we see one." Then Julian tossed his die onto the ground and laughed when it landed with the five showing face up. "We're in," he said.

Rome put his hands on Julian's shoulder and spun him around. "What are you talking about Julian," asked Rome in a slightly aggressive manner. "What's going on? I need more than a simple "follow me". Why are we here at the old library? Who are we meeting?" Julian continued to smile. "What's with that die?" There was no response except that annoying smirk. Rome grabbed Julian's other shoulder and was about to shake him. "Answer me!"

Julian snatched up the die from the ground. "Look, dude. Mr. Jones is gonna answer all your questions. Just trust me, bro. I know it seems strange, but it will all work out. And I'm keeping that Derek Jeter Rookie of the Year card as payment for being your guide."

"Mr. Jones? Who is Mr. Jones???" Rome shrieked feeling that odd burning sensation in his eyes beginning. He had definitely had enough and wanted answers.

"I am Mr. Jones," said a voice from the library doors. A tall and sinuous man appeared in the doorway. "Please come with me, young sirs," he said as he made his way back into the library. Mr. Jones moved towards one of the library desks in the main room. He carefully closed whatever book he had been reading and turned around to face the boys. Both boys made their way into the library and closer to the elderly gentleman. He extended a hand to Rome.

"It's extremely nice to meet you, Rome," he said. His smile was long across his face, and his hand was cold when Rome shook it. He had gray hair, but not much. There was obvious male-pattern baldness, and what hair he had made him resemble an aging Bozo the Clown. He looked Rome up and down, pulling on his spectacles and eventually putting the earpiece into his mouth. "You look great!" he exclaimed. "Almost exactly how I had prophesized you to be."

"Yeah! And he's already started kindling," added Julian.

Mr. Jones abruptly clapped his hands together and smiled ear to ear. "Great Saturn's rings! That's marvelous!" he exclaimed with childlike glee. "We must prepare for The Great Synergy soon. I am sure you have many questions, and I promise to answer each one. But first, I must have a closer look at you. Please come this way." He ushered both boys from the table and led them over to the children's literature section.

Mr. Jones walked around Rome, eyeing him up and down. He extended Rome's right arm straight out and tapped his pointer finger up and down on Rome's wrist. "Nothing there yet?" he asked aloud. He stomped his right foot hard on the ground near Rome's left foot and looked squarely at him. He did it again. He did it a third time using much more force. Each time he stared firmly at Rome. "Hmmmmm. Reflexes are still inert," he mused.

Mr. Jones stared at Rome for a few more seconds chewing on his glasses then finally muttered, "Oh, there you are!" He leaned in closer to Rome and glared decisively into Rome's eyes. "By the Knights of the Round! I see it!" he exclaimed. Then, he moved closer to Julian. "He is going to be very powerful, indeed."

Mr. Jones turned back to Rome and saw the look of a scared cat about to run. His excitement abated. Mr. Jones had allowed his own excitement to supersede the boy's need for understanding. If Rome left now, there would be no getting him back, and another generation could go without having made a connection. He could not wait fifteen more years.

"Please excuse an old man's excitement," Mr. Jones offered. "Rome, do you ever read fairy tale books or fiction of the fantasy vein?"

Rome was bewildered. "Not really," he said, trying to find an escape route. "I watched The Lord of the Rings if that counts." Julian cackled out loud. He exchanged a glance with Mr. Jones, then walked away from the pair towards a distant bookshelf.

Mr. Jones continued. "You see, young Master, most of, but not all of those tales about wizardry and knighthood are very real. At least, they WERE very real in olden times. Especially true are the tomes that pertain to the Kingdom of Britannia and the good king known as King Arthur." He suddenly stood up very straight. "I am going to tell you something, and I want you to please believe me when I tell you this. You are not what you think you are. You are not the normal person you see when you look in the mirror. You come from a long blood-line of great power and tremendous bravery."

Rome cocked his head, not knowing what to expect next. He squinted his eyes and glanced at Julian who was fiddling with his die.

Mr. Jones stepped back and crossed his arms. "You, young Master, are a dragon!"

Chapter Four

Rome stood silently for a few seconds. The thoughts of fleeing intensified. He clicked his tongue with certain verve and fiddled with the zipper on his hoodie. Moments passed before he spoke. Mr. Jones and Julian seemed to be waiting in anticipation.

"So……you are saying that I am a dragon?" he repeated finally. Another few seconds passed. "O-kay. Well, I am going to go now. You two obviously have some things to do, and I have homework to knock out. So, I will see you at school, Julian. Mr. Jones, it was nice to meet you. I will be sure to come by here if I ever have to do a book report on the criminally insane."

Rome started for the door when Mr. Jones swiftly moved to block him. "I know it seems crazy," he said. "But I assure you, what I speak of is true. Please sit and at least here my story. If you still think I belong in a strait jacket, you will be free to leave. There are forces gathering from another realm, and the existence of all living things on this planet depends on a very few select souls. Please hear me out," he pleaded.

Rome looked at Julian who was rolling the die in his hand and staring earnestly. Rome looked back at Mr. Jones who stood with his hands spread wide. "Okay," he said. "But the minute I start to smell hogwash , I am out of here!"

"Very good, young Master," sighed Mr. Jones. "Very good, indeed." He walked to a bookshelf near where Julian was fiddling with his die and cautiously removed a book. He carried it to a table near the computers and motioned for Rome to do the same.

"This book chronicles a very small portion of a history that has long been forgotten. It tells of many battles that were waged between the forces of good and evil. The first of these battles occurred over 7,000 years ago."

Mr. Jones delicately handed the book to Rome, who sat down in a nearby chair. Rome surveyed the book. It appeared to be a short story of about one hundred pages. It was leather-bound and red in color. Rome could tell it was quite old.

He read the title out loud. "Reemergence?" he asked.

"Yes," agreed Mr. Jones. "Included in this novella is the tale of King Arthur's Knights of the Round Table and their battle against an ancient evil that came to Britannia with the intent to destroy their world. It recounts the legend of a tremendously adept family whose destiny was to form a coalition with a powerful ally and defend their realm from destruction. Allow me to expand on this, if I may."

With that, Mr. Jones took back the book and sat down in a chair across from Rome. "I will start at the very, very beginning," he explained. Then he proceeded to tell the legend to Rome. Julian meandered over to the table, but seemed rather uninterested.

"Long ago, before mankind held any power, the Earth was quite different. It was a dark and evil realm. Inhabiting the shadows were several races of creatures who were known as the Darkbrands. These were vile beings that existed only for their own pleasure. After years of fighting and slaughtering, the Darkbrands united under the rule of a cruel and despicable warlord known as The Tyrant King."

"At the same time, living in the mountains was a resilient race of creatures; the Clans of the Dragons. The Tyrant King sought to destroy the dragons because they offered harmony to the chaos of the world. He sent many raiding parties to wipeout the dragon dens, who staunchly kept their independence from each other. A great dragon parley was called when the Clan leaders realized it was in their best interest to unite against The Tyrant King and avoid extermination. There was among them one dragon who took control and united the dragon clans. He became known as The First, signifying that he was the first true leader of the dragons. He was the original dragon lord. However, The First possessed much ambition and sought power as well. His desire was to eradicate the Darkbrands and to claim the entire realm for himself. In order to accomplish his goal, The First decided to destroy the Darkbrands. You see, all dragons, even The First, are born with incomplete hearts. No dragon could ever reach his full potential unless bonded with another entity, completing its heart. The First decided that if he could convince The Tyrant King to bond with him, then he could gain the power to exterminate him and supremacy over the Darkbrands. That would leave him to be the absolute ruler of the realm."

"Little by little The First let it be known that he wanted peace with the Darkbrands. The dragon sent envoys to The Tyrant King asking for a consultation. Spies of the king informed the ruler of The First's desire for peace. The king saw this as a way to gain power over the dragon clans, so he agreed to an audience with The First. The Tyrant King would profess to also yearn for peace. He would consent to the fulfillment of the dragon's desire to bond, while hiding his own evil intention, which was to slay The First. Since bonding of dragon and non-dragon hearts had never been done before, the rulers sent for The Mages of the First Order. These magicians were charged with creating a ritual to unite the rulers. The Great Synergy was fashioned, and since these enchanters held no allegiance to either being, it was pure in its intent and power. The Great Synergy bound both entities to be forever linked by blood and spirit."

"Neither The First nor The Tyrant King could wait to gain control over the other and become the solitary ruler of Earth. As the ritual occurred, however, something unexpected happened. The dragon ruler changed. Not only did he gain his true powers, but also the pure magic of the rite filled his newly completed heart with goodness. The First saw how evil he had become, and that his plan to

rule the Earth was erroneous. Only a just and compassionate being had the right to rule others. As The First's new heart became pure with the magic, The Tyrant King's heart became ever darker. In the next few years, he put his plan to enslave the dragon into motion. But the power of the First was too great. He and his dragons destroyed much of The Tyrant King's army. Since The First and The Tyrant King shared the same heart, the dragon realized he could not kill his bound brother. The First knew he would need to detain The Tyrant King, so he banished him and his minions to The Void. We do not know much about the realm in which, The Tyrant King and the Darkbrands were imprisoned. No living human or dragon has ever ventured into The Void. It was created in an era when magic was the ultimate law of the land. Legend says that it is a place so vile that light refuses to shine. The ground is so foul that nothing grows, and hope does not exist there. "

"It wasn't long after the banishment that The First began to have waking dreams of The Tyrant King. In these dreams, the dragon could see the banished ruler absorbing all the evil in his new realm and gaining power. The Tyrant King was watching through The First's mind for a time and place to re-enter our world. This worried the

dragon. He could not allow The Tyrant King to find a weakness in the barrier between worlds. And so it was with a sad heart that The First decided on another plan. The Dragon Lord would find a cave deep in the mountains and place himself into an eternal sleep, thus keeping all knowledge of the world from the evil ruler. This would disable The Tyrant King, as they were bound in heart and body. His sentence demanded that he would never wake unless The Tyrant King somehow returned to Earth. If that hallowed day ever happened, The First would again fight against the evil he had helped to create."

"With both rulers incapacitated, and a balance cultivated between good and evil, the Earth flourished. All the fairy tale creatures you read about in books thrived on the new Earth. Dragons became the dominant race, and the legend of The First faded into myth. After many millennia, mankind made its claim on the planet. They lived to the South away from the dragons and the mountains they guarded. Both races were respectful of each other, but there was very little contact between them. "

"For hundreds of years the small blue planet lived in harmony, and many believed that

evil had been vanquished from Earth forever, but that was not so. Somehow a bridge was created leading from the dark realm back to the Earth. Rumors of evil beings and deeds began to spread from the East. When the first waves of Darkbrands launched attacks on the races of Earth, the two forces of good once again parleyed. The most noble dragon clans sent representatives to the human capital of Camelot where the good King Arthur ruled his utopian society. Both races agreed that the forces were growing rapidly and needed to be dealt with soon. For years, both dragons and humans fought to protect the lands they loved so dearly, but the dark forces had gained too much power. They were quickly turning the tide of war, and the return of The Tyrant King seemed all but inevitable. "

"It was on a quiet evening in Camelot when an unassuming stable boy sat with a young dragon pondering the means to fight the evil forces that something pivotal happened. Somehow (this part is lost in the texts) the two re-created The Great Synergy that The First and The Tyrant King had performed eons ago. The magical pact released the dormant powers of the dragon by sharing the portion of his heart he needed. Together, bound by blood, these two young warriors led Earth's forces

in what would come to be called the Despot War. The campaign quickly turned as more young knights performed The Great Synergy with the proudest and strongest dragons from the clans. These human warriors became known as Synergist Knights and were revered throughout the kingdoms. Soon, these valiant duos pushed back all of the evil forces and returned peace to the realm. "

"When the Despot War was over, the Synergist Knights and their Master Dragons lived happily together, knowing that their shared heart meant a shared existence. However, with no war, there was not much for the knights and dragons to do. Most of them became bounty hunters and soldiers of fortune. The great goodness that the bond had created was forgotten with the ever-increasing negative reputation of the dragons and knights. Rumors among the humans began to spread about The Great Synergy ritual, and how perhaps this could open the bridge for The Tyrant King to return. Man has always feared what he does not understand. The Good King Arthur had passed away years before, and Camelot was no longer the nirvana he had built. With fear and envy in their hearts, humans began to condemn and hunt dragons. Mankind's numbers had grown so much during the time of peace that the dragons

were simply outnumbered. They had to flee into hiding for fear of persecution. Mankind owned the Earth and kept constant vigil for attacks from the Darkbrands or the reemergence of dragons."

"As time moved on, the remaining dragon clans hid in seclusion far away from the humans. All six clans found refuge from the humans and faded into myth. The ice dragons from the Den of Iglacia fled to the far South where it was too cold for humans to follow them. The Den of Verdana, the forest dragons, hid deep in the primal forests where not even the bravest of woodcutters would venture. The water dragons, which made up the Den of Oceania, swam to the deepest depths of the Earth's aquatic seas. The Den of Gaia, the earth dragons, dug deep underground where they would be safe from harm. High up in the skies, the wind dragons from the Den of Tempestria sought solace from their human hunters. And the last clan, known as the Den of Volcana, concealed themselves in the fiery mountains of the Far North. Here, they stayed for hundreds of years, and eventually became storybook fodder as well. It is said that mankind spread its population to the mountains where the fire dragons lived and drove them out. The dragons themselves were said to be

exterminated, but some scholars believe they simply adapted their hiding techniques."

Mr. Jones suddenly looked up. "That's where you come into play, young Master," he said. "It is my earnest and humble belief that you are one of the last surviving members of the Den of Volcana. I believe that you are a fledgling fire dragon who simply needs to be set free from your human form. You see, I have been working with Julian here since he was very young. I have traced his bloodline back hundreds of years and unearthed his true ancestry. He IS a descendant of The House of Rider. They were the first family of knights that were able to perform The Great Synergy with dragons, thus becoming Synergist Knights. I have already found one half of the puzzle in Julian. I now need to find a dragon. I strongly believe that your "incident" with the match yesterday was the first step in the realization of your potential. A fire dragon's coming of age is called "kindling". With my help, I can set you free, and with Julian, you can defend our realm from the impending attack of the Darkbrands. Please, I need you to believe me."

Rome searched the room for Julian. He studied Julian's face for the slightest hint that this was some kind of off-colored prank. Julian's eyes were clear, blue, and still. Finally, Rome spoke.

"Okay. Let's say I believe you and your little book there. I still have some questions that I want answered before I agree to go any further down this rabbit hole. For instance, I have never heard of these so called Darkbrands, and I have read about every animal on the planet." Rome sneered at Mr. Jones. "Why are they not in any books or wildlife shows?"

"You're not going to have heard of them because they exist only in shadow, dude!" Julian chimed in. He walked over to Rome with clear purpose and stopped about a foot away staring at him strongly. "This is no joke, Rome. We are dangling on a thread here, and we need all the help we can get. You and I have destinies to fulfill that are thousands of years old. If you're not on board then you need to leave now and quit wasting our time!"

Rome, startled by Julian's abrupt ultimatum covered his tracks. "Listen," he managed. "I am not saying you guys are crazy, but I need either some proof or a little more information before I take place in some kind of ritual or whatever you have planned." Rome stood to his full height, trying to look daunting. "Show me what you got!"

Chapter Five

Julian tilted his head and smirked at Rome. He was quite good at that. "Okay," he said. "Let me show you what I can do." Julian stepped away from Rome. He stretched his arms up and did a few deep knee bends. When he was ready, he held up his die so Rome could see it clearly. "Check this out," he bragged.

Julian rolled the die on the floor so that it headed towards Rome's feet. Rome watched it intensely, as it spun. After what seemed like a comically long time, it stopped spinning and came to rest at his toes. For a second, nothing happened, but then the die began to move; chillingly. In a similar manner to the way the match had moved in Rome's hand the previous evening. It vibrated and twitched for a couple of seconds, then stopped abruptly with the number two facing up. A quick shimmer flashed across the die, creating a burst of light. Rome shook his head and focused as something had materialized next to the die. It was a stick about a foot long, complete with tiny twigs branching off of the main plank and a few bright green leaves budding from the tips.

"You see!" clamored Julian. "I made that appear with the help of my magic die. This die was given to me by my father. He said to use its powers to fend off evil. He said it was mankind's last hope. I think he meant to fight off dragons, but after learning from Mr. Jones, I realized that it should be used to defeat the Darkbrands when they attack."

"Sooooo," quipped Rome. "You are going to fight off a thousand-year old, barbaric army of monsters with a twig?"

"No, dude!" cried Julian. "The die is just like you. It hasn't had all of its powers awakened yet. Once we complete The Great Synergy, I'll be able to create powerful weapons that will vanquish even the strongest Minotaur. You see, I can make different things appear depending on which number it lands on. Two is a stick. Three is a frying pan. Four is a paperclip…."

Rome cut him off. "So you guys plan to "awaken" me into a dragon, fix Julian's trinket generator, and fight off an army of creatures that no one can see. This sounds like a really big joke to me. Am I being filmed?" Rome sounded solid, but he was really shaking in his sneakers.

"Again, I assure you we are very genuine in our plans," Mr. Jones reiterated. He chewed on his glasses for another long moment. "Perhaps a test of your own skill will open your eyes to your destiny. Let us convene to the back of the library. I wouldn't want all of these books being burned up like your neighbor's foliage."

The three of them headed out the back door of the library to an area that looked like a parking lot surrounded with trees and a dumpster hidden behind a fence. Rome noticed a circle had been painted in one corner of the asphalt and another one in the opposite corner of the parking area. Mr. Jones escorted Rome to one of the circles. Across the parking lot Julian stood in the other circle tossing his die up and down in his hand.

"Here it comes, lizard boy," said Julian smiling arrogantly. He threw his die onto the pavement where it landed showing a five. The same enchantment ensued from earlier, and Julian stood proudly in his circle holding what appeared to be a child's slingshot complete with projectile pebble. Julian let out a great roar as he placed the pebble in the sling and cocked it.

"For the House of Rider!" he cried. As he did so, he let loose the sling, which in turn sent the pebble hurling directly at Rome. In a heartbeat, the tiny stone was upon him. Rome instinctively raised his arms to cover his face, but knew there was no way he could avoid being plunked in the head. He anticipated the pain and waited. Nothing happened. There was no pain from the impact. In fact, there was no impact.

Rome dropped his hands to his side and opened his eyes. Right in front of him lay what was left of Julian's stone. It was sizzling and smoking as if it had just been hit with a blow torch. He looked at Julian, whose eyes were as wide as saucers.

"Whoooooaaa! Cool," Julian exclaimed. "Let's do it again!" He set another rock into the sling and aimed for Rome's head. "For Camelot!" he shrieked.

"No!" yelled Rome. He ran at Julian out of terror. "Stop shooting at me!" But before Rome could finish his sentence, Julian's slingshot let loose the second stone. This time Rome saw it coming right for him. Before it reached his face, it exploded into a million tiny shards of rock. Rome immediately felt the same burning in his eyes and stomach he had experienced before. He could feel the heat on his face as he leapt at Julian and tackled the boy to the ground.

"Why are you attacking me?" Rome demanded as he rolled on top of the boy. He felt the burning again and the warmth under his eyes. He squinted to try and make it stop, releasing his grip on Julian.

"Dude! Check you out!" laughed Julian as he scrambled to get out from underneath Rome. "You ARE from Volcana. This is gonna be so AWESOME!" Julian yelled.

Rome could still feel the burning in his eyes, but no pain. He stood up and looked at Mr. Jones who had been watching the whole thing with overt amusement. Rome asked aloud, "Did I do that? Did I explode those rocks?"

"Come take a look, young Master," Mr. Jones said. He directed Rome to look into one of the blackened windows that enshrined the brick library walls. Rome walked a few paces to where he could see his reflection in the evening silhouette. What he saw both terrified and amazed him.

Rome's eyes gave off some kind of ambience. As he walked closer, he saw that they were emitting a crimson aura that rose like flames and disappeared into the night sky about a foot over his head. Smoke and embers poured from the aura like two miniature campfires burning from his eye sockets. Stepping even nearer, he saw that his actual eyes had changed. His irises were wide and their color turned from their usual drab green to a deep, blood red. His pupils had also changed to resemble those of a reptile, and his eyebrows had all but disappeared.

"What is this?" he pondered aloud. "What am I?"

Julian quickly had his arm on Rome's shoulder. "We told you. You're a kindling fire dragon from the Den of Volcana, dude!" he said. "And you've got some serious skills!"

Mr. Jones also cried in joy. "By the craters of Mars! Look at you! I never thought in a million years I would see something as remarkable as you. What a specimen! You are a marvelous creature!" He reached out to shake Rome's hand.

Rome quickly snatched his hand away. "I am not a creature!" he said. "I am not a specimen! Don't touch me!" He stood as erect as he could. Then, in a voice not of this Earth, he deeply growled, "Leave me alone!"

His words pulsed with such force that Mr. Jones was pushed back a few feet by the eruption. His spectacles flew to the ground. His hands shook. "By all means, I meant no disrespect," he pleaded. "I sincerely apologize, young Master. I am simply awed and simultaneously dwarfed by your presence. I do not wish to offend you. I am merely overcome with great emotion right now. Please forgive me, young Master." Mr. Jones bowed his head and took a few steps backwards

Julian also backed away, but gave Rome a mischievous wink and smirk. After a few seconds he spoke up. "So, now that you know how incredibly awesome you are, will you perform The Great Synergy with me? I can complete your heart and awaken your powers. Together, you and I will defend this planet from the Darkbrands. We just need to do the ritual, and we can realize our destinies as brothers"

Rome looked at Julian and then back at his reflection in the window. He moved his head side to side allowing the flames to dance back and forth in the darkness. Thinking out loud, he asked, "Can I control it?" He looked to Mr. Jones. "What is this Great Synergy, and how do we perform it? And most importantly, what are the Darkbrands?"

Mr. Jones spoke softly. "I can teach you to control your powers just like I did with Julian. The Darkbrands are all around. They come and go from The Void to our realm through doorways we call portals. The portals are inconspicuous, yet ever-present. It takes a keen eye to spot them." He stood close to Rome and spoke in a defeated tone. "As far as The Great Synergy, alas, we do not know how to accomplish that task. It was lost to the waves of time. We were hoping perhaps you would be the key to the puzzle. So, young Master... Do you hold the answers to our plight or just more questions?"

Rome thought hard for a moment. He bit his lip and paced back and forth a few times. "The stable boy and the dragon were not royalty or nobility, right?" he asked.

"That's right," said Julian. "My great, great, great, great, great, great, great, great grandpa couldn't even wield a sword. He used a common shovel as his weapon of choice. But when he and his dragon were bonded, it became a great spear. That's how he took down so many Darkbrands. He was a radical guy!"

"Maybe the key lies in YOUR commonplace weapon of choice," Rome suggested looking at Julian's die. "Is there anything special about it?"

Julian exchanged glances with Mr. Jones. "Well," he said. "I've rolled this thing over a thousand times, and it has never ONCE landed on one. At first I thought it was dumb luck, but now I think it's because it wasn't meant to. Or maybe it was just not the right time." He paused. "Oh, man! Your eyes changed back."

Rome whirled around to face the window again. Julian was right. His eyes had reverted back to normal. Rome panicked. "Did I do something wrong?"

"No, young Master," Mr. Jones reassured him. "It is all part of the kindling. As you are untrained, your powers activated with strong emotion and protective desperation. I will teach you how to harness that feeling and bend it to your will. We will practice every day after school. Once you two young warriors are bonded, you will be able to change into your true form whenever you are in need...we think."

Rome crossed his arms in defiance. "Every day?" he asked. "Does that not seem like a little overkill?" Then, he had a very pleasing thought. "Does that mean I do not have to do any more homework?"

Mr. Jones chuckled. "On the wings of Icarus!" he exclaimed. "We will begin training tomorrow evening. You boys meet me here." He began walking to the library door. He turned to face them. "Make sure to bring a fire extinguisher."

Chapter Six

Rome collapsed onto his bed. He lay there for a minute or two before flipping onto his back and staring at his ceiling fan. He watched the blades spin so fast that they blurred into the shape of a circle. Apparently, his untrained dragon eyes were not sharp enough to make out and track an individual blade as it spun eternally around.

Rome sat up alertly. Untrained dragon eyes? What was he thinking about? Surely, this was some kind of joke. He couldn't really be a dragon, could he? It went against everything he had ever known growing up. He remembered birthdays and holidays and all the people he had met in his life. None of those memories would ever be the same if this was really true. True? Of course this wasn't true! How could it be true? He wasn't a character in some fantasy novel. He was just a regular boy, and this was rural, backwoods, small town Georgia. Stuff like this didn't really happen; especially not to him.

Strange as it sounded, the dragon idea made sense. All the bizarre thoughts and feelings he had been experiencing became clear if he only accepted the absurd idea that he really was a dragon. Was his whole life up until now a big lie? The past was muddled and the future was dim, but there, sitting on his bed at that moment, Rome had flawless vision. He felt like he was born again.

Rome stood up and walked over to his C.D. player, turning on some music. Music always helped him think. It stood to reason that he had some weighty decisions to make right now. Would he continue down the path he felt compelled to, or would he stick to the ignorance is bliss ideology? Assuming Julian and Mr. Jones were not lunatics, Rome had a destiny to fulfill. What could he do? What would he do?

He closed his eyes and let the music lull him into deep thought. Questions, serious questions flooded his mind. He knew he needed answers. Even if he were to accept the fact that he was a dragon, he still needed assurance that putting his neck out on the chopping block would be worth it. Who could he trust enough to ask? Who would believe him and not turn him over to the men in white coats with large nets? Rome opened his eyes. It had to be Julian.

His fingers flew through the Dampier Middle School phone directory until he found Julian's entry. He memorized the number and picked up his phone to make the call. While the phone rang a few times, Rome nodded his head and tapped his foot to the music still softly playing in the background. Eventually, someone picked up the phone.

"House of Rider," said the monotone voice. "Where valiant deeds rise in the name of Camelot. This is Julian speaking."

Rome was so stunned that he could not even laugh out loud. After a few seconds, he spoke. "Uh, Julian."

"Hey, Rome!" said Julian happily. "I was really hoping you would call, man. So what's up?"

"Well, your phone greeting, for one," stated Rome cracking a gigantic smile.

"Oh, yeah," laughed Julian. "One of the house rules. When we answer the phone, we have to either say that or, "House of Rider. Protectors of the mighty Excalibur." They both sound rather silly, to be honest."

Rome was finally able to laugh. It felt good considering how heavy his mind was at that moment. He was not sure if Julian was being serious or not, but his tone sounded like it was more of a chore than a joke.

"So, you burn anything down at your place yet?" inquired Julian.

"No," said Rome immediately. "I mean, I cannot really control it yet. I have not even really tried."

"Well," mused Julian. "If you want to control it, you have to practice. I can conjure my weapons anytime I want now that I have honed my skills."

Weapons? Rome giggled to himself. "I get it. Like riding a bike, right? Control the bike?"

Julian was becoming ecstatic. "Yeah, but your "bike" has wings and spews fire!" Both boys laughed.

"Julian," pressed Rome. "I want to talk to you about some things."

There was a long pause. Finally Julian responded. "You want to know if it is worth it," he said sternly. "You want to know why you should risk your neck for this world. You wonder if you should just continue on pretending you never knew about the evil that is constantly scheming to invade our home. You think maybe you should just forget you ever found out you are a dragon, and go on with your life. Am I close?"

"Yes," said Rome. "I admit I have been having some second thoughts."

"Rome, I will be completely honest with you," replied Julian. "I don't know if it is worth it, but I know what's right and wrong. The evil gaining strength feels wrong, and I want to make it right." There was another pregnant pause. "I cannot tell you what to do, but I will give you some advice. I was seven when Mr. Jones found me and began teaching me about The Great Synergy. At seven years old, I had to make a decision to disobey everything my father had taught me and live by MY principles instead. I can't imagine what you may be going through, but I want you to know whatever you decide had better be the right choice for YOU. For me, it was not a choice at all."

Rome listened to Julian breathing for a few moments. "So, what do you suggest?" he sighed.

Julian was promptly back giving advice. "I say you turn on some music, lie on your bed, stare at your ceiling, and give this the deepest consideration you have ever given anything in your life. Because, no matter what you decide, you will NEVER be the same again. You can't simply forget what you now know. And YOU will have to live with the decision you make."

Rome sighed again, deeper this time. "Okay," he said. "I will talk to you tomorrow."

"Good luck, Rome," said Julian. "I'll see ya tomorrow at the library."

As the boys hung up, Rome laughed at Julian's arrogance. How could HE possibly predict what Rome was going to choose? Sure, his words had been inspiring, but this was Rome's choice. Julian had even said it himself!

Rome took the strange boy's advice. He turned up his music and fell like a dead tree onto his mattress. He returned his gaze to the revolving ceiling fan and tried to track a singular blade with his vision.

This was a perfect test and comparison to what Rome was going through here. He likened himself to the ceiling fan blade. It couldn't be seen distinctly among the blur that was all the blades whirling around just as Rome did not stand out among the masses as just himself. This was HIS opportunity to be a part of something greater than himself. Rome decided that if he could use his fledgling powers to single out one fan blade, then his decision would be made for him. His destiny would be chosen.

Rome looked hard at the spiraling fan blades and focused his eyes as sharply as he could. They were moving so fast in their circle that there was no way he was going to accomplish this feat. But, still he tried. He held his breath. He moved his eyes so fast in a circle that he began to feel dizzy. He felt the hair on his neck stand up as he tapped into something extraordinary.

Suddenly, he saw it; the single blade whirling around and around. By using his upgraded dragon eyes, he was able to focus on one, individual fan blade spinning at a remarkable speed. It came with a tingling in his stomach like butterflies and a warmth in his eyes.

Rome, exhaled and chortled at the same time. It was amazing. Rome's abilities were certainly growing exponentially. This was not something he could deny. Julian had been dead on. Even if Rome elected not to chase his destiny, he would never be able to forget or reject what he had learned from Mr. Jones and the boy.

Rome continued to follow the fan blade on its supersonic dance around his ceiling. He beamed while he thought about the dragon powers that blossomed inside him. There was no denying them. But he WOULD need to regulate them

This little test had brought another thought to the forefront of Rome's plight. Not only could he not ignore these powers, but also he felt responsible for using them for good; just like Julian. It must have been the imperfect heart that beat in his chest overflowing with possibility and adventure. Rome was different. He knew what he had to do.

Chapter Seven

The next night Rome met Julian at the library, and for the rest of the week the boys worked every evening on Rome's training. The training, for the most part, consisted of Rome clearing his mind of any thoughts and pinpointing it on an object to incinerate. He was developing quickly. By the third day he could change his eyes on command, focus his fire attacks on a target, and dodge Julian's peashooter pebbles. Mr. Jones said his reflexes were becoming like the great Masters of lore. Julian just thought he was lucky.

Over the days, Mr. Jones also expounded on some of the things Rome wanted to know. Since the fall of Camelot many things had changed. The one thing that hadn't changed was that the humans who believed in dragons still distrusted them. But that did not stop the two species from occasionally interacting with each other. Mr. Jones talked about how throughout history, every time someone claimed to see a giant sea monster or strange lights in the sky it was inevitably a dragon trying to go undetected. Rome also learned that the House of Rider was originally the only family that was allowed to perform The Great Synergy with dragons. Somehow, others had figured out a way to perform the ritual as the war dragged on. Perhaps the key to The Great Synergy lay in the mystery of how these other knights performed the ritual.

Rome learned that The Great Synergy was a very serious and rare pact. Julian and Rome would not only share the same emotions and pain, but also the same lifespan. Whatever happened to one would happen to the other. Just like The Tyrant King and The First. They would be brothers of the heart. They would become a Synergist Knight and his Master dragon.

Mr. Jones told Rome about the other dragon clans and their abilities. The Den of Volcana produced only fire dragons, but some of the other dragons had very powerful abilities. When he heard about the water dragons, Rome thanked his lucky stars he was a fire dragon. What a terrible existence that would be! After they performed The Great Synergy, Rome would be able to convert to his true form which would give him flight, great strength, and armor-plated scales encrusting his body. Rome was acutely excited about being a dragon. That was until Mr. Jones began the lessons on the Darkbrands.

According to Mr. Jones, there were three ranks in the Darkbrand army. Garms were black and purple pack hunters about the size of a tiger but much more ferocious. They used claws, teeth, and extreme agility to fight. Though not the strongest of the Darkbrands, a pack of twenty or more could easily handle a solitary dragon. Julian reported that they had rampant, bad breath.

The powerhouses of the Darkbrands were the Minotaurs. They were similar to the dragons in that they each heralded from one element. For instance, the ice Minotaurs were called Glaciataurs, and they possessed similar abilities to the ice dragons from Iglacia. They resembled the Minotaur of myth walking on two feet with a bull head and incredible strength. On multiple occasions, a single Minotaur could go toe to toe with a dragon and knight depending on the element of the combatants. Julian also claimed that they were the "ugliest mothers to walk the Earth".

The final sect of the Darkbrand army was the Nocturn contingent. The Nocturns fought more on their own than alongside the Garms and Minotaurs. They fought for the highest bidder rather than giving full allegiance to The Tyrant King. They were shapeshifting shadows possessing mid-levels of mind control and superb dexterity. From what Rome could see, they were the template for the boogeyman legend. Julian's ad lib about this rank of Darkbrand was not so flippant. "The stuff of nightmares, man," was all he said with a small shutter.

Rome also learned why some humans wanted all the dragons exterminated. The humans believed that when The Great Synergy was preformed, a portal was opened into The Void. Most humans in the know believed that this ceremony could call forth The Tyrant King and/or awaken The First, thus plunging the world into another Despot War. There was no proof of this, of course. It was just one of mankind's attempts to keep dragons from realizing their true power and taking over the world.

One evening on the way home, Julian confessed, "Even my own dad is against the reemergence of The Great Synergy. He thinks we don't need dragons, because it's the humans that protected us anyway. He raised me never to trust a dragon. That just didn't feel right to me. I felt like I needed to find my dragon. I need to be prepared. Now that the Darkbrands are starting to slink back into our world, I feel stronger than ever about bonding with a dragon, to stand against that evil. It is my duty as a Synergy Knight from the House of Rider to battle the Darkbrand army and drive it back to The Void. I just wish my dad could be more understanding so I wouldn't have to hide it. And now a word from our sponsor." Julian quipped, somewhat embarrassed by his emotional revelation.

Rome wondered about his own parents. Were they dragons also? Mr. Jones told him that they probably were. However, since the fire dragons had lived in secrecy so long, they probably did not even know it. Rome felt sad for his parents in a similar way Julian felt sad for his dad. Would they understand or would they be like Julian's father? At least Julian's father could accept the reality of dragons. What would Rome's parents say about his disclosure?

He could just see it. "Hey, Mom. Guess what I found out at school today? I am a dragon.

Yeah, that's right. I am a full-fledged, fire-breathing, gold hoarding, raw meat-eating dragon! No, Mom. You don't need to call Dr. Brown."

In the following days Rome made major strides with his training. The most important jump happened when Julian attacked Rome with two pebbles at once. Rome dodged the first one, but was unable to sidestep the second rock or use his fire aura to blast it to dust. In a last ditch effort, he threw his arm up to block the attack. Instead of the rock striking Rome in the head, it ricocheted off his arm and into the side of the dumpster. Rome pulled his arm away from his face. He was truly astounded. His arm was completely covered with alternating, scarlet-colored dragon scales. Another startling revelation was found growing out of his arms. Starting where his wrist was, there were large, black spikes running laterally along his forearm. They got progressively larger as they approached his elbow. Rome thought they were beautiful.

"That's gonna make it hard for me to buy you a shirt for your birthday," joked Julian.

"Great Gorgon's stare!" cried Mr. Jones. "You've broken through the magical skin barrier! You are developing magnificently, young Master.

Soon you will shed that entire magic spell and show us your true form. I cannot wait for or fathom how amazing it will be! Then we can begin impassioned planning for The Great Synergy."

Of course, they still didn't know HOW to perform The Great Synergy. Julian and Rome were convinced that it had something to do with the magic die from The House of Rider. Why could Julian not get it to land on one? It was a mystery inside of another mystery, but they planned to unravel it as soon as possible.

Sometimes, when the boys were not training combat skills, Julian would roll the die, and using all his willpower, try to make it land it on one. Mostly, his attempts resulted in piles of conjured sticks, frying pans, and paperclips. Rome still wasn't sure how they would win the battle with kitchenware and office supplies, but he had come to believe in Julian and the old man. He respected Julian's constant positivity and relentless quest for training. He appreciated Mr. Jones for being a veritable wellspring of knowledge when it came to Rome's questions. Both of his compatriots encouraged his sluggish transformation and demonstrated great attention to detail while preparing for the inevitable war. They were growing into a team.

On another evening, while Rome was working on perfecting his arm metamorphosis, Mr. Jones spoke with him seriously. "Young Master," he said. "It's time I showed you a portal into The Void. I must warn you that what you will see is not meant to derail your training, but to heighten your cognizance of what we are up against. Please follow me, Young Master."

The two walked around to the front of the library building and stopped where Rome had previously seen the strange marking. Mr. Jones gestured for Rome to walk closer to the inscription. He then removed his glasses and shook them a little. He blew his breath on the glass portions and rubbed them on his sleeve. He handed them to Rome and rubbed his chin with his left hand.

"Put these on and look directly at the portal engraving," Mr. Jones ordered. "It will feel strange, but it will only be temporary, I promise."

Rome reached out his hand for the glasses. He placed them on his ears. As soon as his eyes met the wood, he realized these were no ordinary spectacles.

There appeared to be a large chasm about the size and shape of a manhole in the side of the building. The hole did not lead into the building. It appeared as if Rome was staring into a bottomless, horizontal well. The hole was so desolate of light, that he could not see more than a foot into it. More amazing than its blackness was that the hole appeared to be pulling the light from around its border down into the abyss. Rome squinted, attempting to see down to the bottom. He moved closer, straining his eyes to make out anything in the obscurity.

"Not too close, Young Master," warned Mr. Jones. "You will see the revulsion in a moment."

After a few seconds, Rome heard a low growling. It started as one groan, but soon turned into a chorus of snarls and howls. Accompanying these sounds were the faintest of figures moving within The Void. Rome could see them. Shadows were spilling out from the depths towards him. They twisted and writhed upon each other attempting to fly out of the darkness. Closer and closer they came. Louder and louder they got. So much so, that their shrieks were at a deafening level. Before Rome could turn to run, the grotesque jowls of something evil came within inches of his face. As it lunged out for Rome, intent on chomping his flesh, Rome instinctively fell back on to the ground and curled up into a ball. In his retreat, he threw the glasses towards the door of the library. He screamed so fearfully that nearly scared himself a second time.

Mr. Jones was immediately by his side. "It is okay, Young Master," he said. "They cannot get to you. They are as immaterial here as the effervescence from your soda pop. I just wanted you to see the evil we will inevitably meet face to face."

Rome quickly stood up, brushed the pine straw from his jeans, and looked at Mr. Jones hard. "THAT is what you want me to fight!!??" he exclaimed. "You think we have a shot against something like that?? That thing was pure evil, Mr. Jones! Did you see it!!?? It came straight for my face!" Rome panted and paced in a small circle. "We do NOT have any possibility of beating those things. I mean, what the heck was that?"

"That was a Garm," said Julian quietly. He had apparently come to see what all the commotion was about. "And you're right, Rome. They ARE pure evil. But that's not all." He approached Rome stopping directly in front of him.

"They are fast. They are ferocious. They are driven by a hunger to kill anything they see. They are coming to our world, Rome. They will come in packs and hunt down everyone we care about. They will cover our beautiful blue world with a gruesome darkness, unless WE stop them. I know you and I can do this together." He reached out his hand to shake Rome's. "I believe in you Rome, fire dragon of Volcana. Do you?"

Rome looked into Julian's eyes. He saw the determination that drove Julian to train and fight. Mr. Jones walked over to the boys and readjusted his glasses. "You see, Young Master, until they gain enough power, they are just a bad fairy tale. However, they will come to reclaim the Earth." Mr. Jones stared at the marker on the wall. "I have been given the tool to glimpse into their world. They are bursting to get out again. The most powerful ones have already gained enough strength to materialize for short times in our dimension. So far, their destruction has been kept to a minimum, but that does not mean it isn't forthcoming. We require assistance now."

Julian spoke again. This time with more force. "I SAID I believe in you Rome, fire dragon of

Volcana. Do YOU?" Julian thrust his hand out again towards Rome.

"Okay," said Rome softly. "We will do this together." He clasped Julian's hand tightly. "As a team," he said sternly. "Now that I know what we are up against, we must unlock The Great Synergy and get some serious power!"

The three of them walked back around the library to continue brainstorming. Rome stopped for a brief second and looked back towards the portal. "I will do this," he said to himself. "You will NOT destroy my home! I will burn you to cinders." As he completed this thought, his eyes raged with the fire of a dragon whose home had been threatened.

Chapter Eight

"Have you guys ever thought that maybe there are other books containing clues to The Great Synergy?" Rome asked later that evening. His brain had been going non-stop since the encounter with the Garm. "Maybe we need to be looking somewhere else to find an answer."

Mr. Jones spread his hands. "We have not pursued that avenue of thought, since in the past, we never had a dragon to use in the ceremony. But, Julian is always talking about the fantasy books on dragons and their human counterparts located in the school library. There could possibly be some inkling of truth in these tomes. I am a firm believer that there must be more soldiers for good in this world. Perhaps some of these books are a call to arms. Maybe you boys should do a smidgen of research."

"What are we waiting for?" cried Julian. "Let's go check it out, dude!"

"Tonight?" Rome asked in a tone a bit more anxious than he meant. "You want to go to school tonight and spend hours reading fantasy novels when we could be home sleeping?" He didn't want to admit how exhausting the earlier part of the evening had been. His body ached in places he didn't know he had. He had trouble focusing his eyes, and the thought of spending hours reading caused his head to sting. "Anyway, how are we going to get in? School does not stay open at night. It is not like your favorite fast food place." Rome looked serious for a moment. "You know there has been a bunch of vandalism recently, too. I think they are afraid that someone might go in and wreck the place."

"Why not tonight?" asked Julian. "I mean, maybe we can find out something that helps with the ceremony or something more about my die." Julian held the die up, rotated it between his fingers, and stared. "I think I read a book once that talked about dragons who shape-shift. Isn't that kind of what you do, Rome? I mean, at this point, ANY new information would be really helpful, ya know?" Rome marveled at Julian's enthusiasm.

Rome looked at Mr. Jones, who nodded his head in agreement. For the first time in a few days, he saw a glimmer of optimism reflecting back through Mr. Jones's spectacles. "Don't worry about getting into the building," Mr. Jones began. "I will take care of that. I may not have the strength and ability of a knight or the power and agility of a dragon, but I do have a small part to play in this saga."

The old man smiled, walked towards Julian, and placed his hand on Julian's shoulder. Rome felt the connection between the two all the way across the room. Who knows how long Mr. Jones had been dealing with this growing battle. Rome understood that he had trained Julian from a young age, but how long had Mr. Jones been privy to all the history and concern of the impending invasion? How long had he been searching for a dragon? Was he sure that Rome could do this? He had finally found the knight and the dragon. Now, could he train two selfish teenagers to work as one for the protection of the world? How much had Mr. Jones sacrificed through the years to fulfill a destiny he could not even partake in? Rome admired the man's resolve.

The boys rode their bikes (baseball card in spokes) all the way to Dampier Middle School. It was getting quite chilly in the evening hours.

Rome's mind wasn't on the task at hand as he peddled. He was trying to figure out how he was going to sneak into the house without waking his mom. Maybe he should call her now and tell her Julian had invited him to spend the night. What if she asked to speak to Julian's mother?

Before Rome had time to think any longer on the subject, they arrived at the school. They left their rides on the side bike rack and quietly made their way to the door by the lunchroom. Rome timidly reached out with his right hand. The knob turned sluggishly, and the door opened.

"Hey, what do you know? The old guy did it," Julian said in a voice that was layered in disbelief. Rome pushed the door open and both boys stepped inside. The school was ominous and foreboding at night. Rome had seen countless horror movies that had this very scene in them.

Julian must have been thinking the same thing. "Let's get moving before something jumps out and takes our heads," he said in a half-joking, half-serious tone.

The boys made their way down the hall to the library. It was strange to be alone in the school at night. Rome looked over at Julian, who gave a slight shutter. "This place gives me the willies," he said. "I do not remember the library being so far away." They could hear every single noise as they walked to their destination. Every shadow played upon the walls making the illusion of figures standing there.

At last, the library loomed in front of the boys. The doors, which were always locked, (whether to keep people out or the books in, Rome didn't know), were wide open. Everywhere he looked Rome saw books. It wasn't that he never came to the library, it was just that since his association with Julian, everything held different meanings. He didn't remember it being this immense or being so populated with knowledge.

"What exactly are we looking for?" Rome asked Julian in a hushed tone. "I mean, it's not like there's a book entitled "How to Perform a Century-Old Ritual between Knight and Dragon"." Julian chuckled and looked around stupefied.

"I'm headed to the Hobbies Section," he finally decided.

"What in the world for?" flashed Rome.

"To see if there are any gambling or dice throwing books, of course," replied Julian. "I gotta get to the bottom of this die, man."

Rome took one more look around the library. Where should he start? Would he find books about Camelot and King Arthur in History or Fantasy? Then, he remembered what Mr. Jones had said about some of the fantasy writings. What had he called the books; "A call to arms?" Thankfully, the library had recently been taken off the Dewy Decimal System and rearranged into genres. Fantasy was over by the circulation desk.

When he reached the shelves, he began perusing the titles, looking for anything about Camelot, King Arthur, or dragons. It didn't take long to find several books with titles that gave hope to his search. "Utopian Camelot", "Merlin: Behind the Beard", "What a Day for Sir Lancelot!". He placed these in a pile on one of the study tables and rubbed his eyes. Exhaustion was setting in, and he needed to wake up.

"Hey, Julian!" he called to his partner. "I am going to go grab some water. Do you need anything?"

From somewhere deep in the library came Julian's reply. "Naw, dude! I'm good. Just don't set anything on fire while you're gone. Remember, we still attend this school, dude!"

Rome laughed to himself. His control over his powers was well within check. Julian just liked to rib him every now and then about it. It was another thing Rome liked about his companion. He always kept the mood light. Even in the face of an impassable hoard of evil monstrosities.

Rome walked out of the library and into the main hall. He sauntered to the water fountain and put his lips to the cool, crisp water. After he got his fill of the precious liquid, he took his lips away from the stream and let out a deep sigh of satisfaction. Rome hated water but he certainly enjoyed the way it quenched his thirst. Ever since he had learned of his fire dragon heritage, he had come to enjoy water a little more. He really enjoyed using his eye fire to make it boil and evaporate.

As Rome stood there contemplating boiling all the water reservoirs in the fountain, he felt a slight rumbling in the floor beneath him. He glanced up and down the hallway looking for the source of the tiny vibrations, but the halls were completely empty. Then, the rumbling turned into a legitimate tremor. Rome's entire body was shaking. He lost his balance and fell down. He frantically began searching for some kind of shelter in case the walls imploded. In his panic, he caught a glimpse of a familiar symbol etched into the bottom of the water fountain. The portal shimmered and glowed like it was continually glossing over. Then, it unexpectedly changed. The silver metal surrounding the inscription turned black, and it began to grow. It expanded into a circular form and took on a third dimension. Rome had seen this before. The portal was opening! Rome was terrified to see what was in that pitch black hole

All at once, SOMETHING came through the abyss. A very large shadow flew out of the gaping hole and landed silently about twenty feet from where Rome had fallen. It stood like a statue for a moment, and Rome could see the same pixelating outline of the beast. "A Garm," he thought to himself.

As the Garm shook itself clear of the pixels, Rome began to make out the entirety of the creature. It was nearly the size of a cow but with a wolf-like body structure. Its fur appeared to be a black coat of thick, coarse hair. Intermingling within the black pelt were streaks of what appeared to be dark purple patches. They ran along the side and back of the animal and came to form a design on its face that resembled war paint. Its eyes were sharp and bloodshot against the jet black fur. They were now solely focused on Rome's trembling body. Rome could see the monster's strong leg muscles twitch as it moved its body to face him. At the ends of each appendage were giant catlike paws that made no sound as they padded on the tile. And, of course, each toe possessed a razor-like, claw about the same length and sharpness as a kitchen knife. Its mouth consisted of a strong jawline which came to a pointed end like a canine. Although resembling a wild wolf, it had no whiskers. Instead, there appeared to be five or six, tentacles growing off its snout. They waved around like octopus arms suspended in an invisible ocean.

Rome sat frozen on the floor; too petrified to even let out a sound or a cry for help. The Garm's eyes glowered at Rome. A snarl began to grow in its throat. Then, it let out an unearthly howl, which bared its hideous fangs and two upward-thrusting tusks. AS it roared at him, Rome got hit by the foul breath of the beast. Had he not been so terrified, he would have run away screaming from the retched stench alone. Julian had been DEAD ON in his description of their smell.

    Before Rome could blink, the Garm leapt at him in full kill mode. Rome instinctively threw himself out of the path of the charging brute backing into a row of lockers. The Garm's inability to stop itself from attacking caused it to careen into a row of lockers on the opposite side of the hall. It flopped frantically, trying to get its bearings back. The thrashing created giant dents and its sharp claws ripped cavernous slashes in the lockers. "Note to self, stay away from the claws," thought Rome.

    The Garm righted itself, shook its head, and prepared for another assault on Rome who still cowered against the wall of lockers. Rome's reflexes had saved him from the first strike, but he now appeared trapped. The beast vaulted its enormous body at Rome, teeth and claws ready for an easy kill. Instinct took over. Rome's eyes began to burn and fire engulfed an area of approximately a yard around him, like some kind of fire shield. As his barrier burned, Rome ducked underneath the airborne Garm and slid into the middle of the hallway.

The monster let out a boisterous whelp like that of an injured bear which resonated throughout the hallway. Rome looked back to see smoke and several small fires burning on the monster's face. Again, it shook its head violently and pawed at itself in an attempt to put out the agonizing flames. The tentacles on its snout pulsated violently, and it let out another blood-curdling roar that sent shivers scraping against Rome's spine.

The creature wasn't as slow-witted as it looked. This time the Garm slowly stalked Rome. Pain had obviously made it reconsider the abilities of the prey. Rome backed up as far as he could against the rows of lockers. Foul saliva drooled from the creature's mouth as it slowly hounded Rome with ever tightening semi circles. Rome knew his fire aura was not strong enough to take down this malevolent beast, but he wasn't sure what he could do to stop it. He might have a chance if he could partially morph into dragon. He crossed his arms in front of his face to protect his head and waited for the inevitable onslaught.

Instead, a curious thud sounded, followed by a shriek of pain from the Garm. A frying pan bounced off its skull and landed near Rome's feet.

Seconds later, another metal pan clanged off the beast's skull. Then, another knocked into the massive neck of the beast. Finally, the Garm turned its bewildered attention in the direction of the flying projectiles. Rome cautiously uncovered his face to see what the heck was going on.

To his surprise and relief, Julian stood about twenty feet away with a frying pan in his hand. He continued to roll his die and conjure more pans in a pile on the ground. The whole scene would have been comical were it not for Rome's dire circumstance.

"Leave him alone, fiend!" Julian yelled as loudly as he could. Then he hurled another frying pan in the direction of the Garm, but missed wildly, almost knocking Rome in the shin.

This must have really upset the Garm because it changed its stance to face Julian and his astonishing cooking utensils. From his vantage, Rome got a better view of the monster's true strength and size. The purple streaks of fur spiraled all the way down its body. The hind quarters seemed even larger than its front legs, making pouncing attacks the monster's forte. Its midnight black tail, resembling something from the big cat family, whipped back and forth. "This is the perfect killing machine," thought Rome to himself.

The Garm swiftly sprang at Julian with deadly intent. It landed on top of him, pinning his shoulders to the polished floor. It snapped its awful jaws at Julian's head multiple times, but Julian used one of the frying pans to cover his face and fend off the brute's tusks and teeth. Sparks flew from where they scraped against the pan's metal. It tried to bite from different angles, but the frying pan prevented Julian from becoming a tasty morsel.

Julian screamed and called to Rome for help, but Rome was motionless. It was as if his feet had been nailed to the floor. He watched in horror as the Garm continued its relentless assault on Julian and his makeshift shield. If only Rome could move. If only he could DO something to help his friend. Fear kept Rome immobile. He couldn't do anything to save the fledgling Synergist Knight.

Chapter Nine

"Dude, help me!" screamed Julian. "Rome, please! I don't want to be eaten!" he cried. "Hit it with some fire!"

Something snapped in Rome, and he began to move. He scooped up one of the discarded frying pans and ran up behind the Garm. With all the strength he could gather, he started wailing on the ribcage of the creature. Rome managed to get in three or four hits before the Garm swung its colossal paw at him, knocking him back across the hall. This time, Rome got up quickly, rushed the monster, and jumped into the air before landing his first blow. He came down with the blunt edge of the frying pan hard on the beast's spine. The Garm turned its head, and Rome smacked it right on its nose. The Garm whimpered again and momentarily released of one of Julian's shoulders. Shaking its massive head, the Garm kicked Rome back down the hallway with its hind leg.

This was the break Julian needed. He quickly squiggled out from under the Garm's grip, snatched up his die, and sprinted to Rome's side. "Are you okay, dude?" asked Julian. "That was a great shot. What made you hit it on the nose?"

"It works on sharks, and they are much smarted than our furry friend over there," Rome replied while trying to catch his breath. The Garm jerked its head around, caught in a sneezing fit. The tentacles on its snout squirmed frantically like a disturbed clew of earthworms. Rome wasn't sure if the Garm felt pain, but he hoped that the blow to its nose truly stung.

Julian helped Rome to his feet with his usual smirk. The boys stood side by side, staring at the incredible beast as it turned again to face them. Still smirking, Julian picked up a frying pan and twirled it adeptly in his hand.

"It's now or never, Rome!" whispered Julian. Rome looked intently at Julian. He amped up his eye fire and began to morph. His arms transformed into their armored state faster than they ever had before. "Let's take down this devil!' cried Julian.

Weapons ready, the boys heroically charged the beast. Much to their dismay, however, the Garm shoulder blocked Rome into the lockers and grabbed Julian's leg with its mouth. It dragged him to the ground and started biting his shoe like a dog with a chew toy. Julian tried to pull himself out of the Garm's possession, but his double-knotted shoelaces kept his foot securely in the Garm's jaws. With one desperate arm fling, he threw his die out into the middle of the hall.

"Rome!" he roared. "Become the fire dragon you're meant to be!"

Rome opened his eyes and saw the die tumble across the laminate tiles in what felt like slow motion. He watched intently as it bounced every which way, making trickling echoes in the hallway. He could not believe his eyes when the die ultimately stopped spinning with the number one facing up.

Simultaneously, two things transpired. First, the die erupted in a brilliant, golden light which shot up to the ceiling and expanded outward. The light radiated throughout the school and consumed the three combatants. It was warm. It was powerful. It blinded the Garm so fully that the beast yelped and snarled, biting at the light as if fighting off an invisible assailant.

The second thing that occurred was truly astounding. Apparently, in their dire need, Rome and Julian unlocked the secret of The Great Synergy. The very thing they'd been trying to uncover for weeks now. Immediately, Rome felt a tangible sensation in his chest. It overwhelmed him, and he felt as if he was burning from the inside out. He could feel every cell in his body shifting at once. The glow from the die lifted him off the ground then softly settled him on his feet in front of the cringing Garm. Rome opened his eyes and let his fire signatures burn bright. He turned his hands over and over, watching them change from weak, pale, human flesh into the ironclad gauntlets of dragon hide. His arms stretched out and became the forelegs of a mighty fire dragon.

Rome's eyes burned hotter than ever. Smoke bellowed from his maw. He let out a roar that shook the school's foundations. Scales covered his body. From his back, two magnificent, golden wings sprung forth. Rome carefully moved them as they expanded into their full form. They were breathtaking. He grew in size exponentially while all the scales covering him turned into incandescent rubies. Dark spikes sprouted from his arms and knees. A larger row of them crested his head and ran intermittently down his back to the tip of his muscular tail which extended to the point of becoming quite a formidable weapon itself. Rome was now a dragon.

The warm light from the die abruptly stopped and shot back into the die's one pip. The smoke and fire from Rome's transformation ceased to burn. He was completely altered from the thin frame of a thirteen-year old boy into that of the most majestic, imposing fire dragon the Earth had ever witnessed. At least he thought so.

Rome stood on his hind legs, tucked his wings away, and craned his serpentine neck to find his comrade. He took one long stride towards Julian's exposed body causing the Garm to flinch and back away. Rome reached down with his teeth and carefully grabbed Julian by his shirt collar. Then, he moved the boy behind him out of harm's way and swung his head around to face the Garm.

The Garm growled and bared its teeth to show it wasn't intimidated by the appearance of a dragon. The hair on its back raised, it released an otherworldly howl, instinctively trying to scare off the new, imposing threat. Rome returned the

Garm's challenge by unleashing a deafening roar of his own; revealing his enormous, alabaster fangs. Somewhere deep inside the dragon's chest a light began to glow. It became brighter and brighter until it encompassed most of his torso. Rome pulled back his neck, and with as much power as he could, let loose a stream of scorching fire at the Garm.

The flames spontaneously encased the Garm. It jumped away from the hellfire and rolled around on the ground, extinguishing its blazing fur. While still burning in some spots, the monster lunged directly at the dragon's neck. It clamped its teeth down and clawed at the dragon's sternum with all four legs, like some kind of bizarre necktie. However, the treacherous weaponry of the Garm had no effect on the dragon's enchanted breastplate. Rome swung his neck around, tossing the Garm down the hall like a ragdoll.

Julian had finally regained his composure. "That's what I'm talkin' about, Rome! Send that filth back to where it came from!" he hollered at his friend. Julian was taken aback when pixels began surrounding him as well. "Well, this is interesting," he said to himself as the pixels twinkled around him.

The Garm gathered itself and prepared to launch another attack. This time the dragon was ready for it. The two enemies collided in mid-air and wrestled to the ground. The Garm again tried to bite the dragon's neck, but instead Rome wrapped his tail around the Garm's torso. He squeezed with all his might. The Garm began scratching erratically at the dragon with its every labored breath. A lucky swipe connected with one of the dragon's eyes. This forced Rome to release the monster and recoil briefly. The opening allowed the Garm to jump on the dragon's back, but the defensive spikes that sprouted out of Rome's spine made hanging on difficult. Rome swiveled his head from side to side, releasing a firestorm at the beast. The Garm jumped down from his back to avoid becoming barbecue and spun around to attack again.

This time the dragon's giant claw swatted the demon in mid-flight crashing the Garm against the wall. Rome raised his claw with the intent of smashing his foe into pieces, however, the Garm did not stick around for the party. It dodged away trying to out-flank the dragon. With one swing of his tail, Rome belted the Garm back down the hallway where it skidded to a motionless heap. Derek Jeter would have been proud.

Rome braced himself for another attack, but it did not develop. The Garm struggled to its feet. The animal was limping with one foreleg held at a strange angle, and the tentacles on its muzzle thrashed voraciously. It let out another howl, but this howl was not one of challenge. It was one of apprehension. This fight might be to the Garms death. Its hackles stood up like spikes, but instead of attacking, it disappeared in a flash. Rome growled in misgiving. Something was not right. His fiery eyes surveyed the area like spotlights. He could still feel a dark presence in the hall, but he could not see the hell-spawn.

Suddenly, Rome felt the iron jaws of the Garm clamped onto the back of his neck. Somehow the Garm had moved into striking distance unnoticed. Rome tossed his head back and forth trying to shake the creature off, but the Garm would not relinquish its bite. The dragon extended his wings trying to dislodge it from his neck, but the Garm adeptly dodged his attempts. Rome roared and began spewing fire in all directions. This only succeeded in causing the Garm to bite down even harder, bringing the dragon to his knees.

Unexpectedly, something hit the Garm in its side. It let out a wounded screech and fell over. Once again, it disappeared and reappeared some ways down the hall. Protruding from under its shoulder was a blue steel shaft of an arrow complete with beautiful green peacock feathers. Rome looked behind him and saw something that warmed the entirety of his newly completed dragon heart.

Julian stood tall in the middle of the hallway. He was decorated head to toe in knightly, silver armor that shined gallantly in the vestibule lights. He held in his possession a magnificently handcrafted bow and arrow set. The bow was as large as the knight, but he seemed to have no problem handling it. Slung over his shoulder was a leather bound quiver with an enigmatic emblem sewn into the tanned pouch. The quiver contained five or six more arrows, all elegantly designed with the same green peacock quills.

"Dragon," he said. "Let's show this thing what happens when it attacks our home."

He notched another arrow into the bow and took aim at the vile monster. Rome inhaled deeply, which caused his chest to glow again with the promise of an inferno. As Julian loosed the arrow, the dragon let out a bellowing spire of fire that engulfed the arrow in mid-flight setting it ablaze.

The Garm cried one final roar as if to curse its opponents before the arrow struck right between its squirming tentacles. There was a flash, and then the monster simply ceased to exist. Only an indistinct shower of pixels remained. It was as if the arrow had transported the creature back to the deep, dark emptiness of The Void.

Rome turned his head to look back at Julian. "This is my number five," said Julian holding out the resplendent bow. "Not quite the peashooter you were used to dodging, huh?" he smirked. "Her name is Artemis, and she shoots true every time!"

That was the first time Rome witnessed what Julian's dinky, little die was truly capable of. Well, that coupled with the fact that it had unlocked Rome's full dragon potential. Rome had to admit, The Great Synergy had lived up to its expectations. His transformation was complete. His heart was complete. Just as had Julian promised, he was finally set free.

Chapter Ten

"What comes next," Rome wondered. "Am I going to be stuck in this form forever? I guess there will be no more homework or going to classes. Where will I sleep? Do I NEED to sleep? What about eating? How many cheeseburgers will I have to devour to fill my dragon stomach?"

As Julian sauntered over to him, Rome opened his mouth to speak. Instead of "Hey, Jules! That was a really cool attack," snarls and deep grumbles were heard. Rome was shocked. He tilted his head slightly and stared at his friend.

"Oh yeah. I forgot about that," laughed Julian. "It will take a while for you to regain your human speak while in your dragon form. Mr. Jones mentioned something about that. I would not worry too much about it though. Mr. Jones will assist you with your verbal insufficiencies. You should see your face when you try to talk, though. It is quite hilarious, dragon!"

Rome sneered at Julian and puffed some smoke out of his nostrils. Julian found this hysterical. For all his seriousness, Julian sure had a way of finding the humor in every situation. Rome pointed one of his giant claws at Julian's chest and flicked him. Julian went straggling backwards.

"Whoa! Take it easy!" he laughed. "We shall get you back to Mr. Jones, and he can explain what happened to us. He will be so pleased with what we did here. I can see him now. "By the Towers of Atlantis! Good work boys!" Julian joked.

Rome stared at Julian. He wondered how they were going to get back to Mr. Jones. How do you transport a forty-foot dragon through downtown without arousing some type of suspicion? More importantly, how was he going to make Julian understand him?

Julian stopped and looked at Rome. "Come, dragon. I will change you back. Unless you want to stay like that a while longer?"

Rome shook his head emphatically. He wanted to be back in boy form so he could celebrate the victory with his partner. There was so much to discuss with his cohorts, and he was dying to get some answers. Had they achieved The

Great Synergy? If so, how? Mr. Jones said it was an extensive ritual. Rome felt like they had done it out of necessity. Had they cheated the system somehow? It was now up to the three of them to perfect the harmony between dragon and knight.

"Well, then," said Julian. "Let us head back over to my die and roll it again"

As they walked towards the die, Rome caught a glimpse of himself in one of the cafeteria windows. He stopped briefly to admire the reflection staring back at him. He really WAS a dragon. There was no doubt about it.

Everything he had read in fairytales and seen in movies was there in front of him. With his neck fully extended, he was probably about twenty feet tall. His body was completely covered by those shimmering red scales all the way down to the tip of his tail. His wingspan extended out to about twenty feet across. They were leathery to touch, but shined a brilliant gold. Was he capable of flight? Mr. Jones said he was. Rome was excited to try that out later. He did not have any horns, but the black spikes on his back ran all the way up to the center of his head like a spiny Mohawk. His razor-sharp talons matched the black spikes on his back, legs, and forearms. His eyes could emit fire, and now he knew he could even breathe fire. He was quite a formidable sight; like a colossal reptilian tank. With proper combat training, Rome was sure he could cause some serious damage.

That is when the reality struck him. "Damage? Oh no," he thought. "What about all the damage we have done to the building?" He looked around at the destruction. He hissed at Julian ardently.

"What is it?" Julian asked. "Have you hunger, dragon? We shall get you a big, fat cow to eat, or maybe a half dozen sheep."

Rome was in no mood for jokes. What if the police had even been called? They could be in serious trouble! Rome ran up to Julian and butted him with his head. He snarled a couple more times and stared at the die.

Julian understood. "Okay, okay, okay!," he said. "You do NOT have to be so pushy." Julian scooped up his die and rolled it on the ground. He must have had some kind of control over the die since it immediately landed on one. This time there was no bright light permeating the halls or pyrotechnics emitting from Rome. There was simply a flash and there he stood (fully clothed).

"Oh, man!" wailed Julian. His magical bow and gallant armor had disappeared as well. "So much for getting some target practice in." He shrugged and looked at Rome

Rome patted himself down. He felt back to normal. He grabbed his face, his hair, and (most importantly) his rear end. Everything seemed intact. He even looked at his nails to make sure there weren't any claws instead of cuticles.

Before Rome could expound upon how absolutely crazy it was that he had just seconds earlier been a living dragon, he grabbed Julian and pointed at the rows of lockers. "Jules, look what happened!" he strained. "Our fight DID this! There might be police on the way right now!"

He scanned the halls again looking at all the carnage. At least twenty lockers were smashed in. Quite a few of them had vast claw slashes ripped into them. The cafeteria had two or three broken windows. Some of the tiles of the floor looked like tectonic plates smashing against each other from where Rome had stepped too forcefully. It was chaos.

Julian's eyes got wide and his jaw dropped. "Ooooo-oh my gosh! You're right!" he cried. "We gotta get outta here. We gotta get back to Mr. Jones. He will know what to do. I bet he can even fix it." He grabbed his die, shoved it in his pocket, and took off down the hall. Rome instinctively ran after him heading towards the lunchroom exit. The boys rounded the corner to where Rome and his buddies played hackey sack, but they comically stopped in their tracks.

Two police cars were parked in the side entrance of the school. Their sirens lit up like blue and red comets dancing across the night sky. The boys knew they were in for it when one policeman rapidly approached them.

"Hey, you two!" he yelled. "Stop where you are! Put your hands where I can see them!" The boys accommodated him and stood perfectly still. "What are you doing here?" he asked as he reached them.

Julian spoke first. "We were heading to the school to do some research in the library for a book report," he said. "We heard a really big commotion and decided it was best to get out of there."

"Book report, huh?" said the officer not buying that excuse at all. "Both of you sit over there by that wall now!" he ordered. "Hey, Roberts! You check out the inside. I'll question these two." His partner stepped lively to the door the boys had exited and drew his gun. He tried to open the door, but it was locked.

"Hey, man," said the other policeman. "It's locked!" Rome and Julian peered at each other skeptically.

"Well, force it open," the first policeman replied never taking his eyes off the boys.

After struggling with the door for a few moments, he eventually got it unlocked. He peeked his head in two or three times before he finally slipping inside. Rome could not believe his eyes. They had JUST come through that door.

"We got a call from a concerned neighbor behind the school," the officer explained. "She said it sounded like someone was filming "Jurassic Park" in there."

Julian giggled. Rome elbowed him in the ribs. The officer came over to the boys and got in their faces.

"What's so funny, son?" he asked Julian.

"Nothing, sir" Julian replied. "Uh....It's just ironic that we are doing our report on a book about dragons. I'm sorry, sir." He tried to hide his smile in his chin, but Rome knew exactly what Julian found so funny.

"Dragons, huh?" the policeman probed. "What are your names? I hope you have someone we can call to pick you up after I get done questioning you. There's been plenty of complaints around town about teenagers causing damage and destroying property. Just the other day, we responded to a call that some kids had lit a woman's tree on fire."

Julian burst out laughing. Rome kicked him in the leg and glared at him. He stopped laughing immediately.

The officer peered closely at the two boys and spoke. "You two fellas wouldn't have something to do with that, now, would you?" He pulled out his flashlight and shined it in Rome and Julian's eyes

Before he could go any further with his interrogation, his partner came bursting through the door. "Officer Benton! You gotta see this, sir! It's like something from a warzone in there!"

Officer Benton leaned back from the boys. "You two stay here," he commanded. I'll be right back for you. Duty calls!"

Chapter Eleven

About thirty minutes passed while the boys waited patiently for some resolution. More police cars came and went. The fire department came to make sure there weren't any injured people in the building or fire hazards. Officer Benton stayed near the boys most of the time asking the same questions over and over again. When did they get there? What did they see? Did they have anything to do with the destruction or know anybody that had? They stuck to their lie that they had not even entered the building.

After having seen the carnage first hand, he realized the boys were not suspects at all. He even called Julian's dad after about forty five minutes to come get the boys. He seemed to have bought Julian's chicanery. It made better sense than any other scenari. If they had told him that they were an apprentice mage knight and a shape-shifting, fire breathing mythical dragon defending the town from an otherworldly demon-beast, he probably would have arrested them for being inebriated; or liars.

Before Julian and Rome could get any closure on what the police intended to do with the scene, Julian's father showed up. He walked over to the boys who were now wrapped in police provided blankets. He was dressed in a black suit that looked like something a Disney villain might wear; or a disco dancer. When he spoke, Rome cringed.

"Julian Pellinore Rider!" he boomed. "What do you have to say for yourself?"

What happened next was peculiar. Julian's tone and persona changed in his father's presence. "My sincerest apologies, sir. We are at no fault in this predicament. My companion and I were simply retrieving tomes that we require for a scholastic endeavor." Rome's jaw dropped in bewilderment as he looked at Julian. Julian continued. "My hope is that you and my matron can find in your heart of hearts to excuse my actions. Foul luck has intertwined itself into this miscalculation."

Rome couldn't help but snicker. "Your matron?" he scoffed.

Mr. Rider turned to Rome. "And who is this disheveled young knave?" he asked Julian in a puckish manner.

"Father," started Julian. "Tis a classmate of mine named Rome Lockheed. Despite his personal appearance, he is a close colleague and confidant. He is quite gifted in games of skill and wit. It was my desire for you to grant him audience, but not under circumstances so unfortunate."

Rome was about to burst. Exhaustion was finally catching up with him. That along with the present set of circumstances struck Rome as hilarious. The sheer madness of the situation, mixed with the absurdity of the conversation was almost too much for self-control. He had to hold his breathe to keep from erupting into a fit of laughter. He was sure that Mr. Rider was judging him as "colleague material" by the way he stared at Rome when Julian spoke.

Why was Julian behaving like a complete weirdo? Where did he learn to speak in "Ole English?" Was this how he interacted with his parents all the time? No wonder Julian was so "informal" with everyone else. Rome was drained just listening. Thank goodness he was the dragon, not the knight!

"Well, then," said Mr. Rider. "Allow me to chariot you to your parents. I am sure they miss you by now. Though I would not speculate as to why."

Mr. Rider settled the boys into his car. He drove a pristine, silver BMW sedan that seemed to glide across the asphalt like it was on ice. The windows were tinted so no one could see inside. That was a shame because the interior of the car was as immaculate as the outside. The entire thing was cloaked with silver leather that was cool to the touch and highlighted by golden accents. It contained every possible accessory one could imagine with more leg room than seemed possible from the outside. Rome chuckled when he saw the license plate. It read KNIGHTRIDER. As prim and proper as Mr. Rider appeared, he apparently still had some sense of humor. The car itself truly was a modern-day chariot. Rome tried not to get entranced.

As they drove towards Rome's house, he caught Mr. Rider glancing at him multiple times in the rear view mirror. "Do I know your parents, Roman?" Mr. Rider inquired in a cavalier tone.

Rome spoke softly. "It's Rome, Mr. Rider, and I don't think so, sir. They do not get out much.

We are not real active in the community. Mom works during the day and Dad works on the graveyard shift at the plant. I am pretty sure they are not in your social circle."

The last comment came out sounding more sarcastic than Rome had meant. He hadn't thought about the social differences between himself and Julian. They were not in the same groups of friends. Before the events of the last few days they really had little in common. Now, they shared a heart. Rome wondered what that would mean from here on out as far as public interactions.

Mr. Rider looked at Rome again. His stare made Rome uncomfortable. Rome peered out the window to avoid eye contact with him. This car could not get him home fast enough. When he did finally get there, it wouldn't be for long. He needed to talk to Mr. Jones as soon as possible and that would mean sneaking out.

"Well, Julian," said Mr. Rider to his son in the front seat. "How is your understanding of your armament coming along?"

"Grandly, sir," Julian responded. "However, I would request more time for my complete mastery. In fact, I was hoping to devote the evening hours to practice alone."

Mr. Rider whispered to his son at this point. "Is the commoner privy to what we speak of?"

Julian reacted in shock. "Of course not, father. I would never jeopardize my family's lineage, my family's pride and, most importantly, my father's approval for a fleeting fellowship with a peasant. Long live the House of Rider!"

Mr. Rider smiled arrogantly and glanced back at Rome in the mirror. He seemed pleased with his son's answers. He seemed gracious in his son's discretion. There were a lot of things that "seemed" good about Mr. Rider.

It wasn't long before they pulled into Rome's driveway. "Thank you for the ride, sir," he said as he began to exit the car.

Before he could step out, Mr. Rider swiveled in his seat and grabbed Rome's shoulder. In a tone that was menacing as well as arrogant, he said, "Roman, I would thoroughly enjoy a chance to converse with you and your parents. Perhaps we could arrange to have you for dinner one night. I'm sure you and Julian can mediate an evening rendezvous." He looked at Julian. "Can I trust you to coordinate such an event?"

"Of course, father," replied Julian. "It shall be done."

Mr. Rider looked back at Rome. "Do please stay out of trouble, Roman. I would hate for my son to be involved in anything dubious." He let go of Rome's shoulder and turned back around in his seat.

Rome stuttered. He had the feeling that he had just been dismissed. "Umm. My name is Rome; and, of course, Mr. Rider." He looked towards Julian. "I will see you tomorrow, Jules. Good luck." Rome slipped out of the vehicle.

His goodbye wave was lost on the occupants in the BMW. After they were out of eyeshot, he ran into his house. His mother was asleep on the coach with the TV still playing an old Disney movie. His father had already left for work. How different his family life was than Julian's. Rome's parents didn't have time to be involved in their oldest son's life. They had to trust that he was staying out of trouble, or at least not getting caught for something "dubious". Rome often wondered what he would have been like if he was from the other side of the tracks. In this case, it would have been the other side of the creek. Would he take school more seriously, if college was expected of him? Would he care more about dress, manners, and social standing? Who knows?

Too much had happened tonight. Mr. Jones had been right. He was a full-fledged dragon, and Julian was a knight with magical powers. Together they had beaten a Darkbrand from The Void. There were questions that needed to be answered. Right now, however, he needed to sleep. Mr. Jones could wait until tomorrow. Rome went to his room and dropped down onto his bed. As he lay there waiting for sleep, he realized that his life would NEVER be the same.

Chapter Twelve

The next day came too soon in Rome's opinion. As he opened his eyes, he realized that his entire body ached. He sat up and winced. Maybe a hot shower would help. At least it would give him the opportunity to check for any visible battle scars that required concealing.

Dressed and fed, Rome practically flew out the door. Both boys' bikes were still at the school, so Rome would be walking today. He hoped that he could see Julian before classes started. When he approached the school, Rome saw Julian standing on the front steps.

"Hurry up, man," Julian yelled. Rome broke into a trot. He met the other boy and they started into the building. "We have to get our stories straight. It's already all over school."

"What is all over school?" Rome asked.

"Everyone knows we were here last night. We left our bikes in the rack, and the damage to the school can't be denied. I foresee us spending some time in Mrs. Case's office today. We should make sure that our stories match as much as possible. We won't be able to pull much over on her. She has a keen ear for BS." They only had a few minutes, but followed the same story line they had given the police and Julian's father. When the bell for class rang, both boys were satisfied that they had a 50-75% chance of pulling off the scam.

The entire school was abuzz about what had happened in the main hall. Most students thought some construction crew came through and destroyed the place with heavy machinery. Others whispered about a movie being filmed in their school. Rome's favorite hypothesis was what Clay said in the hackey sack circle. He thought some animal activist group had freed some elephants and lions and let them loose in the hallway. Police tape streamed across the cafeteria windows. Orange cones and police wire prevented at least fifty kids from getting to their lockers. There were all kinds of tile workers and carpenters on site trying to get the school back into working order. Until then, there would just HAVE to be some misplaced students. The county could not possibly let them have a couple days off of school. The show must go on, as they say.

Rome could not focus on his classes. There was just too much to think about. He wanted so badly to change into his dragon form and practice his new powers. In fact, he even thought about transforming and scaring Mrs. Fillbin half to death when she called on him unexpectedly in Geometry class. Rome knew he had to keep his new powers under control. He knew he had to use them for good. His battle was with the Darkbrands, not The Quadratic Formula.

As the day wore on, nothing happened. The boys would pass each other in the hallways, nod, and keep moving. Spending time together would only add fuel to the verbal fires. Let's face it, Rome was not quite ready to start any new fires just yet. Both boys were looking forward to getting to the library tonight to brainstorm with Mr. Jones. They had many questions to ask him about the Darkbrands and the portal in their school.

At one point in the day, Rome ran into Julian at the water fountain where they had first exchanged uncomfortable, yet epic words. Rome looked below the fountain and saw the same symbol there. It still shimmered. It was still open, apparently.

"What are we going to do about this?" Rome asked Julian while taking a long drink. "Is there any way to seal a portal so no more Darkbrands can get out?"

"Honestly," Julian confessed. "I don't know. We need to ask Mr. Jones when we get there tonight. Maybe he can use his glasses somehow to shut it down. I mean, I remember him saying that the portal outside the library is no longer a threat. He must have some way of doing it. Maybe the secret is in his magic glasses. Oooooohwaaaa!" Julian put his fingers to his eyes imitating someone with glasses and shook his head about.

"Can you be serious for one minute?" asked Rome. "If there's a way to shut down a portal BEFORE anything comes out, we may not have to do as much fighting. I cannot speak for you, but my body is killing me from last night's funfest. Plus, I think we got lucky with that one. These things are serious. It was like a tiger on steroids!"

Just about then, a girl walked by and stared at the duo. Julian quickly opened one of his books and began pointing at the page. "The answer is right here," he said in an overstated voice. "You need to pay better attention in class, Rome. Geez!" Julian chuckled nervously. The girl shook her head and continued on. Julian closed his book.

"So much for the invincible fire dragon of Volcana! Don't act so weak, dude. You and I together can handle ten Garms at once," he scoffed. Julian smacked Rome on the shoulder. "We just need to keep training. However, I do see your point. We should definitely ask Mr. Jones about it tonight. Anyway, I'm heading to my last class, but I will see you as the evening falls upon us." He spoke the last part in a manner similar to how he was speaking last night. He made a silly face and tapped his fingers together. Obviously, even he could laugh at how nonsensical he acted around his father.

"Yeah, yeah. Of course," muttered Rome. He bent down to take another peek at the portal on the fountain. It still shimmered when he looked at it meaning it must still be active. He hoped Mr. Jones knew a way to prevent a reemergence from the portals. How many were there? Were they all centered in Canton, Georgia? Well, that didn't make any sense. If there were portals all over the world, how were he and Julian supposed to stop the flood of evil? What were the chances that there were other knights and dragons to help stem the tide from The Void? Thoughts whirled around and around in Rome's mind. School dragged on.

As the final bell was about to ring, a knock came on Rome's classroom door. A student aide with a note stepped in and gave Rome a look of the deepest sympathy. Rome's teacher took the note, read it, and sent Rome with the aid to see Mrs. Case. There was no conversation on the way to the principal's office. Rome entered the waiting room and sheepishly sat down in a rough chair. He wondered how long he was going to be there. At that precise moment, the door to the office opened, and Mrs. Case emerged, followed by Julian.

"Thank you Mr. Rider for your cooperation," hummed Mrs. Case. "I will be keeping a close eye on you for the rest of the year." She laced her fingers and turned to Rome. "Now Mr. Lockheed, please come in and take a seat. Let us see what you have to say about the unfortunate incident from last night."

Rome stood and gave an inquisitorial look to Julian who stared back blankly. Rome entered the office and sat in the chair in front of Mrs.

Case's desk. Mrs. Case followed him and seated herself at her desk. She moved some pencils around on her desk and closed one of her drawers tightly.

Rome had never been in her office before. It was comfortable. Comfortable was the right word.. The walls were a soft blue and covered with degrees and personal pictures. There were bookshelves with all varieties of books. The throw rug gave the whole room a finished look. There were even fresh flowers on the side table by the navy couch. The interrogation chair wasn't too uncomfortable either. Mrs. Case herself, seemed to fit the décor perfectly. All in all, the entire office exuded warmth and affability. This really put Rome's senses on high alert.

"Now, Mr. Lockheed, what do you have to say for yourself?" Mrs. Case asked in a charismatic voice. Thus began the longest twenty one minutes of Rome's life. He told the story that he and Julian had agreed upon. She asked questions, and he answered them always sticking to the truth whenever possible. He wanted to tell her the truth. There was something about her that made him feel protected. She didn't berate him for answers, but rather sweet-talked them out of him. In the end, she seemed satisfied.

Mrs. Case stood. "Thank for your help with this situation. You and Mr. Rider seem an odd pair to me, but I believe there is more here than meets the eye. I will be watching. Good day, Mr. Lockheed," she said. For the second time in less than twenty four hours, Rome felt like he had been dismissed. He rose and left the office. Mrs. Case was strange. He was going to keep a close eye on her too.

Rome rode his bike home. It felt good to be out on his own and away from school with time to think about the recent events. He was still a little bit in shock that he was actually a dragon. Teenage years were hard enough, but now he had to deal with this? Things in his life had taken a serious turn in the last couple days, and he would need to figure it out soon.

When he got home his mother was waiting. "Hello, Rome. Where have you been? I missed you last night. What time did you get home from your homework session?" she inquired.

Rome sighed. It was time to weave another story. He just hoped that he could keep all the threads of his story web straight. Maybe he should write down who he told what to. It would surely help keep everything in line. He really needed to tell someone the truth. It was time to see Mr. Jones.

Rome finished his homework (blah) and jumped on his bike to head to the library. When he got there, he was a little confused. He walked in the front door, carefully eyeing the portal on the left, but could not find Mr. Jones or Julian anywhere. He walked up and down every section of the library. He checked both bathrooms and even scoured the parking lot out back. Could they be hiding in the dumpster?

Rome stopped in his tracks halfway to the dumpster. He heard noises faintly in the distance. He quickly located where the sounds were coming from and turned to face the dark woods behind the library. He could hear intermittent yelling and what sounded like Julian screaming. Was his brother in trouble? He had to help him.

Before Rome even thought about what he was doing, he took off running through the woods towards the sounds of Julian's voice. He rushed past pines and spruces as fast as his legs could carry him. He was in such a hurry to save his friend that he was only looking straight ahead. Right before he got to a clearing, his shoe got tangled in the root system of one of the massive oak trees living on the border of the woods. He lost his balance and was unable to regain his footing. He came crashing down face-first into a mud puddle about three feet inside the clearing. Rome had no idea what he was about to face, but he knew he had to get up and help his blood brother. He had to help his knight. He forced himself up from the ground and yelled for Julian.

"Well, would you look at that," came the reply. "Mr. Jones, when was the last time you heard of a fire dragon playing in a puddle? That's not something you see every day!" Rome spun around to see Julian bent over laughing and pointing at him. "Are you sure you're a fire dragon? You look more like a mud dragon!" he cackled.

Mr. Jones approached Rome with a towel. "Here, Young Master," he said calmly. "Clean yourself up. We have been waiting for you to get here to continue training. I heard about your encounter with the Garm, and I must say I am utterly impressed. I cannot believe you two have completed The Great Synergy. This is a most marvelous day!"

"What were you doing running through the woods like a crazy man?" asked Julian. "We would have waited for you, ya know."

"I heard you yelling," explained Rome as he wiped his face. "I THOUGHT you might be in trouble. I was coming to help you, and I guess I tripped on that root."

"Running towards unknown danger to help your comrade?" inquired Mr. Jones. "You probably didn't even stop to think about your own safety, did you?"

"Well, no. I guess not," admitted Rome. "I just thought Julian was being harmed, and that I needed to save him." Rome looked at the ground. "I guess I should not be so reckless."

"By the light of The Golden Fleece, no!" cried Mr. Jones. "You have taken the first step by conducting The Great Synergy. Your bond with Julian will only continue to grow. You innately realize how connected you two are. What you share is more than a friendship. You are blood brothers! Your fates will be forever intertwined and your lives forever linked. The fact that you were willing to charge blindly into battle to aid your Synergist Knight shows how far you've progressed already. A completed dragon's heart bears much more love than a human's. You truly are amazing, Young Master." He looked at Julian. "Julian is overly so lucky to have you."

Julian put on a sour face, crossed his arms, and kicked a rock. "Yeah, yeah. Let's get down to business, old man. You wanna see this or not?"

"By all means," said Mr. Jones. "I have been looking forward to this for countless years. My Lords, if you will. Please fulfill an old man's lifelong dream."

"Is this clearing gonna be big enough for you?" asked Julian. "We decided to move out here away from civilization. After what you did to the school, we figured we'd need more room to train."

As Julian dropped the die to the ground, Rome quipped, "You helped me make that mess, Jules. Did you tell your "matron" about that?" Julian gave Rome a quick smirk and then stepped a couple paces away from him. Rome WOULD need some room to show his true form to Mr. Jones.

The light from the die exploded as it came to rest on the number one. The luminosity filled the entire clearing. It was so thick that the golden glow seeped deep into the woods; zig-zagging between the trees. The glen held an aura of sepia with things moving in slow motion. It was as if Rome was watching a film showing on an old fashion projector. He couldn't focus on anything or anyone. Within seconds, Rome's vision cleared. He was amazed at the sharpness of his sight. He could see objects that should have been too far away, and the evening darkness appeared to have little effect on his ability to see accurately. Night vision! He found it interesting that he could not remember this change last night. Come to think of it, Rome bet that there would be a lot of alterations that he would not remember from last night. During the battle, he was too involved to notice the amazing effects that were happening to him.

Mr. Jones was not. He fumbled with his glasses obviously startled by the brilliance of the golden light. He strained to see through the steam and smoke that accompanied the change. His glasses became smeared with dust and particles of clinging matter. The more Mr. Jones fidgeted with his spectacles, the worse his vision got. It was as if something was keeping him from seeing his greatest desire. When it cleared, and the smoke faded away, Mr. Jones stared in awe. Rome had been transformed into a perfect specimen of dragon. There was no description in any fantasy novel that did him justice.

Rome stared down twenty feet at a visibly stunned Mr. Jones. "Great Gaia's grandchildren," the older man whispered. "Young Master, you are exquisite." Mr. Jones became so filled with emotion as he walked closer to Rome that he quivered. He extended a trembling hand towards Rome's forearms. "May I?" he inquired. Rome nodded in approval and wisps of smoke escaped his nostrils. Mr. Jones cautiously ran his fingers along Rome's scales, from the bend in his forearm to the tip of his claws. "It's absolutely amazing! I never thought to see this day. What a marvelous dragon you are Rome; perfect in form and stature. " he said almost reverently. "It's incredible! No it is beyond incredible. It's historic!"

"Yeah, that's exactly what I thought when I saw him last night...historic." jibed Julian. Mr. Jones was so engrossed in the dragon that he failed to notice Julian as he approached from the rear. As he turned to take in the boy/knight, Mr. Jones clasped his hands together and applauded like a small child on Christmas morning. Julian had also transformed into his Mythril armor; this time complete with a helmet. He took the helmet off. "Nice duds, huh? A little heavy but sure shiny. Hey, speaking of shiny, do I have to polish these or will they always appear like I just picked them up at the cleaners?" That was so Julian, always bringing sarcasm into the conversation.

Mr. Jones circled the knight. He inspected the various parts that made up the armor; pulling and tugging on it. He banged on the chest plate so hard that it knocked Julian back several paces. "Hey, what gives, mage?" Julian said. "How come you did not bang and pull on the dragon like that?" Rome gave several little snorts that almost sounded like laughter.

"Well," Mr. Jones replied. "I have never seen a dragon before. I am not completely sure where they ... ah, fit together. But a knight's panoply, now that is something I understand. Yours is fine, just fine!"

"Great! The dragon is historic and I am just fine. Change into a dragon and get all the attention. Just my luck," Julian snickered.

After several more moments of intense investigation of both dragon and knight, Mr. Jones took a seat on a nearby rock. "Now, it is time we talk about last night," Mr. Jones said in that teacher voice he often used when he lectured. "I need to hear it all. Don't leave anything out. Some detail you consider minor, could be of utmost importance."

Julian jumped in with both feet. "How do we kill these things? Last time we got lucky. How do we seal a portal? The one in our school has to be plugged or some serious harm could come to the people in this town."

Before Mr. Jones could answer, Rome who had been enjoying the banter between the two humans, lowered his head to their level. He wanted to tell the story from his perspective. Instead of words, however, low pitched rumbles and snorts came out. He knew the words he wanted to speak, but his dragon vocal cords could not be controlled to voice them. A feeling of aggravation began to form in his belly. It was strange to feel emotions in his gut instead of his head. To ease the feeling Rome let out a cloud of steam aimed at Julian

"Oh yeah," said Julian looking at Rome with annoyance. "I was getting to that. How do we fix the dragon's speech?"

"Well," explained Mr. Jones. "He can never speak human while in dragon form. There has been a barrier preventing communication between the races since biblical times. Humans used to communicate with dragons through a form of writing, but that language has been lost. You might say it is like Latin; a dead language. However, once knight and dragon are bound with The Great Synergy, the two parties can converse by telepathy. Have you two tried linking your minds?

Dragon and knight stared at each other and concentrated. Flashes of thoughts raced through Rome's mind. He twitched unexpectedly. He tried to grab hold of one thought to see if he could make sense of it. "This is crazy," Rome mused. Julian's thoughts were not words, but more like pictures. Rome opened his mind and allowed more pictures to flow freely into it. He was inundated with visual flashes of cartoon characters and skateboarders performing tricks and juicy hamburgers and constant barrages of video game scenes. All at once, he came to a place that was quiet. It was peaceful and dim.

"Have you made the connection?" Mr. Jones asked. Both nodded. "Now, imagine this space of your collective minds is like a mental chatroom or text message thread. Here you can visualize your thoughts and communicate with each other. Eventually, if the bond between you grows strong enough, you will be able to materialize these thoughts into real dialect, so you will hear rather than see. Through enough practice, you will also be able to talk out loud by using this shared power. It is called "spatial linking". There is little known about its limits, but some former Synergist Knights and their Master dragons used this to predict enemy moves and coordinate joint attacks. Some regiments from Arthur's army claimed they could even use it between multiple heroes. It allowed for entire phalanxes to fight in concert. It is like having a telepathic connection that is much more intimate than social media. It is quite special."

"Great," said Julian. "We must to learn how to talk all over again. That should be easy enough. Now, teach us about closing the portals, and how we destroyed that Garm."

Mr. Jones inhaled sharply and reached for his bag. He opened it and pulled out the book.

"It's all in here," he said. "I will continue to teach you everything I know, but I must warn you that not everything will be as easy. You did not perform the rite of The Great Synergy, but somehow you bonded last night. We must make sure it is an eternal bond. One that cannot be broken. We need your combined powers to defend our people. These are desperate times and they will require desperate actions."

"Sure, old man," quipped Julian. "The dragon and I can handle it. We are brothers until the end. We will defend this realm, and we can read each other's thoughts, now!" He turned and looked up at Rome. "By the way, dragon. Cecilia Parker is waaaaaaaay out of your league." Rome blushed redder than his scales.

Chapter Thirteen

The knight began the tale of the previous night's clash. When the deeply embellished saga was finished, Mr. Jones told them that, at this point, the Darkbrands were still not "technically" alive on our dimension. The energy they had been saving up for hundreds of years allowed them passage into our realm for limited amounts of time. So, while they seem real enough, and can cause physical damage to our planet, they eventually run out of energy and are cast back into The Void.

"That explains what happened to the Garm you faced yesterday," clarified Mr. Jones. "It's not that you killed it. Your attacks exhausted the energy it had saved up, and it was simply sent back to The Void. For now, the Darkbrands are doing basic reconnaissance and scouting through these portals. When The First exiled The Tyrant King and his followers, it was foretold that the only way they could permanently return to our existence was if

The Tyrant King returned to his throne. So he and his minions have sat in darkness for hundreds of years collecting enough power to make his return possible. His last attempt was thwarted in Camelot by the dragon and human coalition, but he is always growing more powerful. He is obsessed with returning to his once glory and constantly trying to get back to his former home. We cannot allow that to happen. So we will prevent his minions from arriving here and stirring up trouble. We will guard and destroy portals that we find."

"Okay, so how do we destroy portals?" asked Julian. "Rome and I can see them. You can see INTO them, but we don't know how to seal them."

"It takes a special and strong magic to seal a portal. I do not have this magic myself," admitted Mr. Jones. "I have exhausted my supply over the years."

Rome wanted to speak, so he went into the spatial linking with Julian. Julian read his thoughts. "Rome wants to know how you sealed the one by the library."

Mr. Jones cleaned his glasses. "A very good question, Young Master. That was actually sealed by my predecessor, Mr. Smith. You see back in Camelot, the good King Arthur had a wizard named Merlin who helped him. Although many thought Merlin to be a powerful sorcerer, he was really just a modern day magician that had a few relics containing enchanted properties. The lens in my glasses comes from a shard of a magic mirror that allowed the ancients to see into The Void. My predecessor modernized it for function and fashion reasons." Julian chuckled. Mr. Jones ignored him. "So, as Arthur had his Merlin, there has always been what you might call "guides" to aid in the battle for Earth. It's not a family thing. It's doesn't matter one's lineage. There just needs to be someone to help teach and direct the forces of good. My teacher, Mr. Smith, cast a sealing spell on that portal by the library and sacrificed himself to shut it down forever. Now he is trapped, you see. Trapped in the darkness of The Void for eternity as well." He paused and looked into the distance. "The evil that grows in that darkness takes from everyone. Even me."

Rome concentrated on the spatial linking. Julian spoke for him. "The dragon wants to know what sacrifice it would take to seal the portal at our school. He says he has no problem sacrificing me." Julian spun around. "Hey, dragon! Not funny!"

Mr. Jones and Rome snickered. "The answer to that escapes me as well, Young Master. For as much as it would quiet my days, I would not even want to sacrifice Sir Julian. He has been a valuable companion and apprentice over the years."

Rome concentrated on the spatial linking harder this time. Something happened. As Julian was relaying Rome's question, Rome also began communicating out loud.

"Now he wants to know…..uh. Mr. Jones? He speaks."

In fact Rome was speaking from his dragon mouth. "Dracul gaun ronle ponchu donrar galla," Rome spoke in a deep, gruff dragon voice.

Mr. Jones grabbed Julian by the arm. "Can you hear it, Julian? He's speaking to us in the dialect of the eternals. He is speaking drake tongue!" Mr. Jones and Julian looked at each other. "Can you translate using the spatial link?" asked Mr. Jones.

"I don't think so," said Julian. "It's coming across as that weird language in my head."

Rome continued. "Trallon havar pol ursten pronteel. Caraunt nergil fo tum grava that I am able to change when Julian rolls the die?"

Mr. Jones leapt into the air. "Holy Lancelot! Rome, you are speaking English! You have already mastered the spatial linking enough to allow us to hear your thoughts. Look how you move your lips too! How swift you mastered that! It took some dragons years to develop that ability." He looked at Julian. "Do you know what this means? You two are way more advanced than I could have ever predicted. Your bond is growing exponentially by the hour. You should try your die again, and see if your power has grown as well."

Julian glanced up at Rome. "Of course he is "advanced". Just look at who you paired him up with. I'm the best, and since you don't need me anymore to translate, I think it is time I practice my crap shooting!" He winked at Rome. Rome puffed some smoke.

Julian left them to converse and walked off to experiment with his magic die. Rome took this opportunity to finish what he was asking. His voice was intense and thick. "Mr. Jones. If this is my true form, how come we have to roll the die every time I want to change into it? Shouldn't it be the other way around?"

Mr. Jones approached the majestic dragon. "The secret is that you are under a spell cast by your ancestors," he said. "When the Den of Volcana fled from the mountains, they realized they would need to be among mankind to avoid persecution. One of your forefathers crafted a spell that would conceal your true form from the world. They must have set it mark your entire family tree and every generation thereafter. Whereas the Talisman provides Julian with magical enhancements, for you it removes them. Hence the beautiful vision I see before me. My advice to you would be to stay in your concealed form unless we need it. I do not think the world is ready for the reemergence of dragons yet."

Rome nodded in agreement. "Mr. Jones, I think our focus should be on getting the portal at my school permanently sealed. How can we find a spell strong enough to do that?"

Mr. Jones chewed on his glasses. "I do not know, Young Master. "Perhaps the secret lies in the House of Rider. It seems we have exhausted our knowledge on my end. Were you able to locate any information in your school's library?"

Rome shook his head no. His school library catered its fiction section to the young adult audience as opposed to children. Fairy tales weren't popular with 8th graders. Rome knew there could be plenty of clues in books spread across the world, but the time it would take to search every book and decipher what was real and what was fiction was an unimaginable task.

Mr. Jones spoke as if reading Rome's mind. "We will have to stick to what we know is applicable. The House of Rider is our only concrete lead. If we are to seal the portal, we must trust that Julian's family archives have the answer."

"How's this for an answer!" barked Julian emerging from an ample pile of frying pans. He strolled over to his friends carrying his latest mystical accomplishment. It was a large heater shield that covered Julian's entire torso. Much like the Artemis, this shield was absolutely stunning to look at. It was encrusted with blue gems that surrounded the entire border. There were myriads of shades of gold and red that formed a cross pattern on the front. Directly in the center was a picture of a holy woman. Encircling her were several sunset colored barbs. In the epicenter of the women's breast was one larger iridescent spike extending out about six inches. The shield looked to be wooden but was reinforced with some kind of metal bracing. The type of artistry that it took to produce a guard like this no longer existed in this world. Aside from its painstaking design, Rome also sensed an unusual feel to it as if it was protected by magic.

Julian stopped a few feet from his companions and thrust the shield into the soft ground. "THIS is my number three weapon of choice," he proclaimed. He raised the shield over his head proudly. "This is Pridwen!"

Mr. Jones and Rome were quite impressed. Rome had never seen a medieval shield in real life, and this masterpiece was well beyond magnificent to behold. He seemed to recall reading about a shield with that name in one of the parallel readings for World Literature. Something about King Arthur and some battle. "Pridwen! I have heard that name before. Did you name it or did it come with a tag?" Rome rumbled.

Julian looked like his feelings were hurt. "This is Pridwen, the legendary shield of King Arthur. It is said that he used it in the battle to defeat the Knight of the Burning Dragon. It kept the Knight's blade, which supposedly spouted

Dragon Fire, from harming King Arthur." Now he sounded like he was bragging.

Julian's grandstanding gave Rome a mischievous idea. If the legend of Pridwen was true, could it defend Julian against Rome's dragon fire?

Julian looked up at the dragon nervously. "Wait a second, dragon" he stammered. "We don't really need to test it, do we? I mean, it's a mythical shield of lore. I know it can protect me against the strongest elemental attacks."

Rome was surprised that Julian had read his thoughts. "I say we give it a try anyway," growled Rome with a toothy grin. He planted his feet firmly on the ground and inhaled sharply. The scales on his chest began to glow while Mr. Jones eagerly retreated behind the tree line. Rome was ready to fire.

"Hey hey hey, man," pleaded Julian. "It's cool! You don't need to do that, dragon! Calm down! We can just..."

Before Julian could finish his thought, Rome was blowing a stream of fire in his general direction. Instinctively, Julian lowered himself to one knee, hiding his face and arms behind the shield. Rome's conflagration continued for a couple seconds, and the shield lived up to its legend. Pridwen repelled the flames, which veered around the cowering knight and flowed like comet tails on the all sides of the shield.

Rome stopped his assault. Julian was still huddled behind his shield screaming in fear. Once he realized he was no longer in danger, he jumped up and rushed Rome. He got right in the dragon's face and began shouting any obscenity he could think of at him.

Mr. Jones benevolently intervened. "Gentlemen that is enough horseplay. We need to develop a plan of action soon. I can tell the Darkbrand army is getting stronger with each foray into our domain. We have to seal that portal before more venture to our realm. We cannot constantly be there to defeat them if they come through. "

Julian calmed down, understanding the severity of the situation. He rolled his die which landed with the one pip facing up. The Great Synergy flashed and changed the boys back into their civilian garb. "I guess we will have to ask my dad," he shrugged. "He does not know that Rome is a dragon, so he won't be upset. We will just have to tell him that Rome was with me when we came across a Garm, and that I defeated it before it could do too much damage."

"You're going to say you defeated a Garm with frying pans and paper clips?" Rome asked in disbelief.

"Sure," said Julian. "Why not? My dad will be super proud of me! Or I could tell him the truth, get my best friend possibly killed, and worse yet, get myself grounded for life."

Julian's logic was sound.

Chapter Fourteen

With renewed ambition, the boys cruised to Julian's house at top speed. The idea of traveling by dragon had appealed to both of them, but Mr. Jones had suggested that perhaps it was a little early to be flying over the Georgia countryside. His logic was also sound.

Rome was always impressed when he saw Julian's house. It could be seen from two streets over. The front stairs ascended from both sides of the driveway. Ornate wasn't a strong enough adjective to describe it. The railing was a bright gold color. Rome didn't think it was real gold, but after meeting Mr. Rider, he wasn't so sure. The steps were made of fine Italian marble with a flicks of gold metal sprinkled inside. Rome was very careful as he scaled the palatial staircase. He didn't want to be accused of trying to mine gold from the marble. That kind of thinking doesn't inspire confidence, not even in oneself.

At the zenith of the stairs was the massive entry way to Case de Rider. The actual doors were heavily carved and made of what looked like mahogany. Julian turned the gold doorknob and pushed the doors open, exposing the foyer and smaller, identical staircase on the left.

"My house is a little different," Julian stated almost embarrassed by the opulence. He was right. Rome had been in some museums that were smaller.

They walked into the foyer and through a doorway to the right leading to what could only be a guest receiving room. The room was large and lavishly decorated. There were gold-colored, velvet couches and matching loveseats. Opposite of these, were old-looking, ornamental chairs. An enormous bearskin rug held the place of honor directly in the middle of the room. The skin was massive; stretching all the way to the brass fireplace. A fire burned brightly in the hearth adding a touch of warmth to the extravagant room. Rome liked that.

He walked to the fireplace and began looking at the pictures on the mantle of various Rider family members. There was one of Julian and his father, one of an older gentleman circa 1930s, and several others dating around the turn of the century. There was one particular picture that caught Rome's eye. It was of Julian and a young girl. The picture was apparently made quite a few years ago as Julian could not have been older than eight or nine. He wore a pastel blue tunic with a yellow undershirt. He also wore what looked like a bow tie and a blue cape. His hair was almost white and stood up in spikes. Just barely noticeable in the picture, behind his shoulders, was a spout of hair called a rat-tail. It was a horrible, short-lived haircut popular with unruly kids in the late 80's and early 90's.

Rome laughed and pointed at the photograph. "Who is that little dork in that picture up there?"

Julian gave a sigh of annoyance. "That's my younger sister, Camela. She is away at boarding school."

"No, not the girl," chuckled Rome. "The one with the cape and ponytail?"

"Hey, man," started Julian. "That picture was taken for my mom's birthday! Besides, now that I'm a Garm slayer, maybe I should break out that cape again."

From behind the boys, someone cleared his throat. The boys turned around to see Mr. Rider standing at the door to the room. He swirled a portion of red wine in a crystal clear glass. Ironically, he was wearing a cape.

He took two large steps towards the boys and said, "Julian, I thought you were studying your craft? And I see you are still gallivanting around with your unkempt associate." He looked at Rome. "How are you, Roman?"

Rome frowned for a second. "I am great, sir. How are you? This is a lovely room. Where do you keep the coffin?"

"Aaaah the humor of the peasants," remarked Mr. Rider. "What are you lads accomplishing this fine evening?"

"Hark, Father," said Julian back in squire mode. "Mine companion and I bring great news of victory. The previous eve when you collected us from the learning institution, we regrettably WERE involved in mischief. On that night, we encountered one from The Void. You have my sincerest apologies for my dishonesty, sir, but my reasons were just. The encounter left my acquaintance quite petrified, so I needed to minister to his fears before bringing you this news. That is the sole reason behind my deception."

Mr. Rider sighed heavily and sat down in one of the chairs. He swirled his wine again and crossed his legs. "What of the dark one?" he asked.

Julian quickly knelt down before his father. With his eyes glued to the rug, he continued his report. "I fell the beast by my own hand, father. My powers have grown significantly. But for the circumstance, I had to expose them under the watch of a peon. Again, my most genuine apologies, sir."

"Well, I guess it could not be helped," said Mr. Rider after a few moments. "What else have you discerned about our family, Roman?"

"Other than the fact that your interior decorator has a thing for gothic, European castles, not much" said Rome. "And once again, my name is not Roman!"

Mr. Rider looked through Rome unfazed. He sighed sharply and switched his gaze to his kneeling son. "My highest praise to you, Julian for defeating one from The Void. However, deceit is

NOT one of a true knight's qualities. As punishment, you shall lose your privilege to play with your marionettes for one week. I hope you understand the consequence of your actions." Mr. Rider turned his attention back to Rome and spoke with disdain. "Roman, I cannot fathom how your home is run, but I would implore your parents to do the same."

Before Rome could make a joke about how much he would miss playing with his marionettes, Julian resumed his discourse. "Father, I have many a query for you at this time. The Darkbrand appeared from a portal in my educational institute. I fear harm could come to other students and faculty unless we seal it. As we are not as learned as you, could you enlighten us on how we can accomplish this goal? Please, I beseech you!"

Mr. Rider stood up from his chair as if rising from a throne. "You will find in time, Julian that your concern for the common folk will undoubtedly lead to your undoing. However, I cannot have Darkbrands showing up whenever they choose under my watch. Come! Let us hasten to the study." With that, he turned allowing his cape to catch the air and strutted for the room exit.

The two boys followed Mr. Rider up the smaller staircase and down a very long hallway. Rome strained his neck to see into as many rooms as possible, although most of the doors were tightly shut. Rome's mind spun imagining all the creepy and delirious things that may be hidden behind those doors. Julian was quick denounce Rome's fabrications over the spatial linking.

When, at last, Mr. Rider stopped at a door, he turned to the boys. "Many secrets can be found in this domicile. My family takes its traditions very seriously. I trust that wandering eyes will remain firmly set on our objective?" He glanced sideways at Rome.

"Oh, yes, sir," Rome stuttered. "I will not tell anyone about your mortuary."

Julian nudged him. "Enough," Mr. Rider commanded. It was funny to Rome. He was usually very respectful and courteous to adults. It was like some of Julian's personality was coming through in him. It must be another side effect of The Great Synergy.

Mr. Rider opened the door and led the boys into a small room with yet another giant fireplace. In front of this fireplace was a smaller wolf skin rug.

What was it about using dead animals as decorations that the Riders found so enticing?

The fire roared brightly. It made Rome slightly jealous because he wanted to burn like that fire. He missed his true form. This whole parody of Julian getting rid of the Garm by himself did not sit right with Rome. They were a team, and he wanted everyone to know the feats they accomplished together. Well, maybe not everyone. He hadn't quite figured out how he was going to convey this news to his parents.

"Exactly! Now you see what I'm facing," Julian's voice spoke in Rome's head. "My father knows all about knights and dragons. You would think telling him would be easy, but it isn't. To him you are a peasant and well below my family's nobility. Not to mention you are actually a dragon. If he realized that I had performed The Great Synergy with a dragon, he would ground me until the next Haley's Comet, which would leave you ineffective as well; the double whammy. Just be cool and we will figure out both of our problems together."

"Sit down," demanded Mr. Rider. "What I am going to give you boys can be used ONLY ONCE and then never spoken of again. But first, since my warning of mixing with those of inferior breeding has fallen on deaf ears, I must ask a question. Roman, how much of this chronicle do you know?"

The boys sat next to each other on the settee. "That is not my name," Rome whispered to himself. Then after a quick mind meld with Julian, Rome took a deep breath and replied, "Gee, Mr. Rider, all I know is that Julian and I ran into some kind of hideous monster. You know, the kind you see in horror movies with purple fur and spikes and gnarly teeth. It could jump a mile, and if it had not been for Jules here, I would have been wolf food. How did it get here? How did Jules stop it? Did I dream it?"

Mr. Rider slowly turned to his son. In hushed tones, he said, "Perhaps next time you should use Roman as bait. It would alleviate our troubles presently AND in the future."

Mr. Rider walked over to a shelf on the back wall. He returned with a box which appeared to be made of concrete. He opened the top slab and placed the box on a table. Delicately, he withdrew the contents. He placed it next to its container on a white cloth. The object looked like some kind of Halloween decoration or prop found at a magic shop.

"This is the mummified dragon's claw," said Mr. Rider. "Tis the left claw and forearm of a water dragon who died centuries ago. He was one of the last truly heroic dragons, before they all revolted against the human contingency. His name was Leviathor from the Den of Oceania. It has been preserved and kept for generations in our family. My father charged me to guard it as did his before him back through the years."

Mr. Rider paced the room while he continued. "You see, gentlemen. Our ancestors learned In order to close a portal, one must combine a sealing spell with a great sacrifice. Leviathor and his knight Sir Baldwin knew this to be true. When once they happened upon a portal in the evergreen woods of Camelot, they made a blood-brother pact. Sir Baldwin would give his left hand as the sacrifice to combine with the sealing spell. This would in turn close the portal and keep out the Darkbrands. However, since dragon and knight shared the same blood and mind due to the blasted Great Synergy, Leviathor also lost his claw that day. Both warriors decided that with the portal closed, they should keep Leviathor's arm in case the portal should ever open again. And so it was bequeathed through the generations to be used in a time of grim emergency. I believe that the time is upon us. I have had a strong foreboding feeling recently. My dreams have been troubled with visions of the Darkbrands and malevolent dragons. Something is stirring in The Void. It is my paragon and curse to be able to feel the energy from The Void. I can almost see The Tyrant King rousing in his heinous kingdom. If he finds enough energy to bridge the distance between The Void and our world, we will be forced into another arduous war. This time however, we are not organized. We are ill prepared and have few allies. The dragons have thankfully disappeared into legend, and humans have forgotten the magic needed to defend our realm. I will entrust this relic to you under the promise that it will be used for shutting the portal that invades your school."

Rome felt the hair on his neck prickle and the burning in his stomach begin. He was tired of being insulted. He was going to give Mr. Rider a piece of his mind. "What about dragons? Are they not your allies? Why do you hate dragons so much? Have you ever met one? What gives you the right to say dragons are malevolent? In all the books I have read, dragons are wiser than humans," Rome ranted.

"Dragons are a very dangerous race," Mr. Rider replied. "Little is known about what they are capable of. However, we do know that they tricked man into performing The Great Synergy so that they could complete their hearts and become powerful enough to take over the Earth. Once our ancestors had defended the realm from The Tyrant King's incursion, the dragon dens saw their opportunity to become rulers of the land. Mankind could not allow that to happen to our planet. In fact, some human blood oaths go back many generations stating that if humans were ever to meet a dragon sympathizer, they should be exiled from the human ranks." Mr. Rider looked briefly to the floor. "It is a hard truth many have faced."

After a brief pause, Mr. Rider looked sternly at the boys. "NEVER trust a dragon," he said. "Even the great dragons like Leviathor had evil intentions, I'm sure. If you ever have the unfortunate pleasure of finding one, I would suggest immediate eradication. They may have been our allies in the distant past, but I hold them in no higher regard than the revolting, filthy beasts from The Void." Rome clenched his fists. He could feel himself slipping into the dragon mindset.

"Hold it together, dude," Julian warned in Rome's mind. "This isn't the time. We need to learn as much as we can from my dad. We can't alienate him now."

Mr. Rider's tone lightened somewhat. "As for the sealing spell, I have some bottled up in the garage. You simply need to uncork the bottle so its contents can permeate the area of the portal infection and throw Leviathor's claw in once it opens. That will satisfy both needs for a sealing spell and a great sacrifice. I trust even the most meager halfwit can assist my son in such a task." Again he glared at Rome.

Rome was thinking of something else he would like to throw the claw at when Julian interjected. "Of course, noble father. My cohort and I shall rid our realm of that stench that is The Void portal. Trust in me father, for I so desire to regain the use of my praised marionettes. Thank you, sir, for divulging such information to me and for providing me with a means to honor our family name in history."

"Good, son," soothed Mr. Rider. "Now, go make us proud. For the House of Rider!"

"For the House of Rider!" echoed Julian.

As the boys left the main hall and came to a spiraling staircase that Julian said led to the garage. Rome followed Julian down but had something on his mind. "Jules, can you always hear what I am thinking?" he asked aloud.

"Most of the time, I can't. But when you're angry, your voice is louder in my head than my own. I'm sorry that my father is such a tool," Julian said. The boys walked on each immersed in his own thoughts.

When they got to the bottom of the stairs, Rome was confused. This wasn't the same garage Rome had been in earlier. It wasn't even really a garage by definition. It was an unfinished room with grey, concrete floors and alabaster, brick walls. Organization was apparently an afterthought in the storage space. There were shelving units stacked up in multiple corners of the room containing all sorts of what Julian considered to be junk. Large and small boxes populated the room's floors. Some were closed while others were wide open for perusal. There were heaps and piles all over the place of what could aptly be described as clutters of "stuff".

Who knew what treasures could be found down in the "garage" of the House of Rider? There were probably all kinds of magic artifacts and weapons stashed amongst the so called junk. Rome hoped to spend a few hours looking through everything. He expected to find something useful in their fight against the Darkbrands, but that was not in the cards. Rome had just started sifting through the contents of a large box labeled in black marker, when Julian grabbed a bottle from the shelf. He slapped Rome on the shoulder.

"I got it," he cried. "Let's get outta here! We've got some work to do, dude."

Chapter Fifteen

The boys sped as fast as they could to Dampier Middle School with salvation in hand. They were both excited to plug the portal once and for all. The idea of any more of those horrendous creatures spilling out into their school filled Rome with grave concern. Mr. Jones was right. They would not always be there to intercept any interlopers from The Void.

There was little conversation on the trip to the school. The boys' thoughts were personal and seemed to be kept that way. Every so often, Rome would search with his mind finding Julian deep in thought. He didn't intrude. Linked as they were, he could have, but he wanted to respect Julian's privacy. Do unto others...

Upon their arrival at school, Rome spoke for the first time. "I just want to keep our school and town safe," he said to Julian. "I have not been able to sleep very well the last couple of nights because I keep thinking something will come through and attack the innocents of this town."

"I know, brother. I'm super excited to fight for our world, but it would be impossible to guard the portal all the time. The Garms could do some serious harm even if they are not at full strength yet. It's our job to cork this portal for good!"

The boys walked through the door and into the main hallway, surprised once again that the door was unlocked. The school was still a wreck. So many contractors, construction workers, and metalworkers had been coming and going. The boys thought it would be cleaner than it was. They could still see traces of the Garm's handiwork throughout the hallway. It almost looked worse than when the damage was originally done. The officer was right that night when he said that it was like a warzone.

Julian was still looking around when Rome announced, "There it is." He pointed to the ill-fated water fountain. "So, how do we know that it is open enough to throw Leviathor's claw into it?"

Julian looked dumbfounded. "I guess... I guess I hadn't thought about that. Isn't it always open?" he asked to no one in particular. "I mean, if these things come and go as they please then it

SHOULD be opened, right? Maybe the sealing spell opens it? Yeah, I'm sure that's what happens. The sealing spell causes the portal to open, so we can throw the sacrifice into it."

Rome prayed that Julian was right. It would sure be a huge waste of a mummified dragon claw if he wasn't. "Okay, Jules, but do you think we need to transform just in case?"

"I think we should be ok," Julian reassured him. "We should only change into defender-mode if something was to come through. You open the bottle and let out the sealing spell. I'll throw the claw when I see it working." Julian suggested.

Rome held the bottle by the very tip. He was fully anticipating another one of those unholy beasts to pop out any second. He could still remember the smell of the last Garm's breath. It had smelled like old cheese. Rome shivered. It took all his self-control not to throw the bottle at the portal and run for cover. How would that look to Julian, who was standing there straight as an arrow holding an embalmed dragon claw?

Julian read Rome's thoughts and came across the spatial linking. "Don't worry, dude. I'm going to run too as soon as I pitch this claw. I'll beat you out the front door. Remember, my mile time was the fastest in the school last year."

"I remember," Rome thought back. "You had posters printed with your picture and your time on them. You must have hung hundreds of them around school. What a nerd!" This intimate touching of minds gave Rome the courage he needed to complete his task. He wasn't going to let Julian down. He decided they were more that bonded knight and dragon. They were friends. This friendship was something that had to be protected.

Rome tiptoed all the way to the water fountain. He made sure the strange marking was still there, shimmering. Rome shook the bottle a little for good luck. He removed the cork and pointed it at the portal. Blue and purple smoke billowed from the bottle and drifted into the air. The smoke glittered as it danced around the fountain almost like it had tiny fireworks exploding inside its nebulous. As the boys stared awe-struck, something strange happened.

The smoke began to churn like a small tornado down towards the bottom of the fountain. The tornado swirled faster and faster. Something was happening at the portal entrance. A strange howl commenced vibrating through the school.

"Great," Rome thought. "What is happening now?" He looked back at Julian who answered with a worried stare.

"Rome," called Julian. "The portal is opening again. See I was right! Now is our chance!" The howling became louder and louder. Julian yelled, "I'm gonna toss the claw! You need to get back in case something crazy happens!"

No one had to tell Rome twice. He stepped away from the fountain without taking his eyes off it. He found a pile of scrap metal from the locker reconstructions and hid behind it.

The howling was earsplitting now. Rome grimaced and grabbed his ears. As he stared from his hiding place, he saw the one thing he dreaded more than anything. Two dark, imposing shadows flew out of the portal and whizzed around the hallway. Rome got the distinct impression that they were looking for something or someone. He was fairly sure he knew who. Finally, they landed in the middle of the hall. The shadows shifted into the forms of two snarling Garms. They couldn't have been more than twenty feet from Rome. Rome's breath caught in his throat. His heart was beating rapidly and sweat began to seep from his pores. He couldn't move.

"I'm here, brother. You are not alone. We beat one before we knew what we were doing. We're smarter now. We can handle two." Julian's voice broke through the panic and, Rome nodded in agreement. Whether it was a fool's confidence or not, at least Julian never let on that he was intimidated.

The howling stopped and everything was still again. The Garms immediately started snapping at each other and shaking off the pixels that outlined them. They were just as ghastly as the previous Garm. Within seconds, their bodies had completely formed, covered in matted twists of fur that stunk up the whole hallway. The Void must be a truly dark and wretched place all the way at the bottom. No wonder the Darkbrands wanted out so bad.

One of the Garms spotted Julian, who was frozen in place. It barked at the other Garm, in some form of eerie communication. The second Garm shifted its body and turned in Julian's direction. Realizing the Garms were ready to attack, Julian took action. He ran in the direction of the dissipating sealing spell smoke.

"For Camelot!" he screamed loudly, and he threw dragon claw into the swirling smoke and shrinking portal. With an agile change of direction, he ran down the hall towards the cafeteria shrieking like a banshee.

Rome watched from his hiding place as the claw hovered inside the dimensional portal for a few seconds before it shattered into dust. Simultaneously, the portal closed, and the sealing spell smoke disappeared into the void. It was like water going down a drain. It collapsed upon itself around and was sucked into the black. Had it worked?

There wasn't any time for Rome to waste on contemplating the fate of the portal. Both Garms had galloped after Julian with their teeth ready to feast. They raced like rabid dogs. As they took the corner where Julian had last been seen, they knocked into each other, causing both to go sprawling across the floor. One Garm got up quickly and shot down the hall after Julian. The second one got slowly to its feet and followed suit. Rome knew Julian was going to be in trouble unless he could perform their transformation spell. Would they always have to use the die to transform Rome wondered, or would he someday be able to transform on command. Was he magical enough to delete his concealment spell?

Rome jumped out from behind his barricade and started after the Garm. Then suddenly, he saw Julian running towards him from the opposite direction. Julian had looped around the cafeteria and was headed back to his starting point. Rome couldn't help but smile. It always helps to know the lay of the land.

"Rome!" he called. "Get ready, man! I'm coming in hot!" A loud crashing noise came from behind Julian. The Garms came racing around the corner. It would have been comical if the situation hadn't been so serious. One Garm was covered from head to claw with the khaki colored paint the school used on its walls. The other was dragging a fifty foot, orange electrical cord which was tangled high up in its tail. It was obvious that Julian had led them on a merry chase.

Julian reached into his pocket and pulled out his die. He fumbled it in his fingers, and it fell to the ground. To make matters worse, he accidentally kicked it across the floor into the mass of metal where Rome had been hiding. Julian did not break stride as both boys watched the die vanish into the debris.

"Find it quick!" Julian yelled as he ran past Rome. Julian took the turn again and departed down the hallway for lap two. Thank goodness he had the fastest mile time in the school. For him, this was just like track practice. Both Garms went flying past a stunned Rome desiring only to hunt down Julian. How stupid where they?

"Rome, find the die!" came Julian's thoughts. "I'm wasting my fighting energy running around the school like this. I think I am going to need it for the battle to come."

Rome quickly ran over to the pile of rubble and began searching for the die. When he saw a frying pan in the pile, he knew he was close. He threw some junk out of the way and spotted the die.

By the time he had it in hand and turned around, Julian was screaming down the hall towards him again with the Garms gaining rapidly. Apparently, they weren't as stupid as Rome thought. It only took one lap around the school for them to get their footing on the slick, linoleum floor.

Rome shouted, "Catch, Jules!" as he tossed the die to Julian who caught it in his left hand. This would be the part in a movie where everything moved in slow motion; not in real time. With great dexterity, Julian switched the die to his right hand, rolled it on the ground, and slid through Rome's legs. Rome saw the die land on one, and he smiled bravely.

That warm, encompassing light flashed immediately from the die. The Garms came to a skidding halt, temporarily blinded by the miraculous brilliance. They whimpered and their tentacles squirmed furiously. In a second, they found themselves nose to nose with the fiery eyes of a dragon from the Den of Volcana.

Rome inhaled and felt his chest glow red hot. He let go a stream of fire directly at the two shocked Garms. The more adept monster was able to dodge to the left, but the slower one was engulfed in a wave of orange and red. It rolled around on the ground trying to put out the dragon fire. When the flames were out, it stood back up and slowly stepped backwards sizing up its opponent. The other Garm came to flank the burnt one on its right. They were cautious of the dragon, but they didn't seem surprised to find him there. It was if they were expecting to see him. Still they exercised precaution in their approach.

Rome rose to his full height. He expanded his wings and let out a reverberating roar at the two appalling creatures. The dragon had come to fight. He was aware of the Garms' formidable claws and teeth. He knew that they could move without being seen. Rome knew all their tricks, and he was ready for them.

Within a dragon's breath, Julian was by his side dressed in his knightly regalia. He held Artemis, with a notched arrow pointed directly between the burnt Garm's eyes. His armor shined heavenly in the incandescent lights of the school. Sir Julian was ready as well. Dragon and Knight versus two lowly Garms. It almost didn't feel fair to Rome. Too bad, so sad he thought. They were in a standoff of mythic proportions. The only questions was, who would blink first.

Chapter Sixteen

"Rome," Julian thought. "We need to get these guys out of the school so we don't cause another huge mess. I sure don't want to try to explain to Mrs. Case again how I'm not really involved. She creeps me out. Why don't we feign a retreat outside? I'm sure they will follow us. They are not the sharpest teeth on the sawblade. We can lead them into the woods where the battle will be away from prying eyes. Plus any damage can be someone else's problem."

Rome already knew what Julian was thinking. The bond between brothers was exponentially stronger when they were in their battle forms. As Rome began to reply in the affirmative, he noticed something different about Julian's appearance. He swung his great head around and saw his knight had donned a repulsive, olive-green cape. All he could think was, "Where did you get that cape?"

Julian looked over his shoulder and frowned. "Who made you a fashion critic?"

This minor break in the standoff was the invitation the Garms needed to begin their attack. Before they could pounce, however, Rome grabbed Julian by the ugly cape and began to run for the cafeteria door.

"Size," Rome thought.

"Size? What do you mean by size," Julian replied while bouncing around in the Rome's toothy grip.

Rome was incessant. "The door in the cafeteria. I will never fit through it at my current size. I will take out the entire wall if I try. Not to mention what will happen to you. That shiny armor might protect you from Garm fangs, but I doubt it can take the pounding you are going to get when I careen into the walls."

Julian was one step ahead of him. He slung Artemis over his shoulder and pulled out his die. He rolled it into his other hand just as they were about to smash into the exit. It landed on the one pip in Julian's upward facing palm. With a bright flash, the boys changed back into their original forms. Their momentum carried them tumbling through the door as Julian rolled the die back into his other hand. It landed on one again, and the boys changed back with Julian still hanging from Rome's mouth. Rome flipped Julian in the air who somersaulted twice, arms flailing. Somehow, Julian landed safely on the dragons back amid the rows of defensive spikes. Julian screamed in fright, but once he realized his safety, it became a triumphant cheer.

"That was awesome, dude," gasped Julian. "I didn't know you could do that. If everything else falls apart, we can always join the circus. I know I would pay to see that."

"I didn't know I could do that either," thought Rome. "But if you think that was gnarly, hold on to your helmet, we are about to go airborne."

Rome felt Julian dig his knee into his back. Rome ran as fast as he could. He didn't know how but he knew he needed to open his wings. He felt the air rush under them lifting him slightly off the ground. He pumped his wings several times and lifted his massive legs up. The next thing he knew, he was in the air. The dragon and the boy inside him finally felt free. Free from the hold of gravity;

free from the hold of other people. Rome beat his wings and climbed into the air. This was what he was made for. This was what he could do. He did not have the foot speed, knowledge, or cunning that Julian had, but nobody else could fly.

As the dragon circled the school, Julian looked back to see if the Garms had taken the bait. They were running at full sprint to keep up with the dragon. Rome and Julian were cruising into the wind about thirty feet off the ground. The fire dragon could really move for his size.

"Rome," Julian thought. "Try to stay out of view of people. Fly over the woods if you can."

Still getting the feel for flight, Rome veered left. His right wing skimmed the tops of the trees, shaking the dragon and making the knight hold on for dear life.

"Careful, dude. This dragon-riding is risky business," Julian thought.

"Would you rather walk," Rome inquired? "I am just getting the hang of this myself. If you must know the truth, you are causing a massive itch in the center of my back. That armor of yours is downright irritating. Hold on I am turning left to avoid the main street."

Unfortunately, the new path took the dragon directly above Rome's neighborhood. In fact, he ended up soaring straight over Mrs. Baskin's house. As luck would have it, the lady herself was out watering her withered, scorched Crape Myrtle. Hearing the sound of his massive wings, Mrs. Baskin looked up. Rome winked at the old lady as the two made eye contact. Mrs. Baskin let out a small whimper and fainted.

"Alright, Rome," Julian laughed. "You got her again!" The two soared to the clearing in the deepest part of the wood where they had recently trained. As soon as Rome found an appropriate place to touch down, Julian jumped off his back.

Almost immediately, both Garms exploded through the woods into the clearing. They stopped abruptly when they saw their foes in the middle of the field. The Garms slowly stalked towards their adversaries. The tentacles on their faces writhed, and they made guttural growls at the knight and dragon.

Julian pulled Artemis off his shoulder and notched one of his silver arrows. "Fire arrow, dude!" he messaged to Rome.

"No, knight. If we miss, we catch the whole place and surrounding woods on fire," said Rome aloud. "We will have to do close quarter combat this time."

Julian frowned at Rome. "But Artemis never misses," he stated. The feeling Julian got from the dragon said he would not change his mind. He would not ignite any arrows within this woods. Rome's thoughts showed concern for the abundance of innocent life that could be lost by an errant, burning arrow. It may not be human life, but it mattered just as much to Rome.

"Okay. Then it's time for Pridwen," bellowed Julian. He rolled his die and the resplendent shield manifested in his hands. "I guess I'll take the ugly one?" There he was again trying to be funny in a quite serious situation. Julian slowly paced behind his shield staring at the Garms who were now snarling menacingly at the duo.

Rome unfurled his wings. If he could injure one, then Julian could dispatch that one without the dragon's help. That would leave only one full strength Garm for Rome. He was fairly sure he could handle it. Using his wings for speed, Rome leapt at one Garm. Much to his surprise, both Garms rushed at him. Rome caught one with his claw by the face and pinned it to the ground. The Garm screamed and squirmed in the dragon's grasp. This opened the dragon's flank to the other Garm. The second one leapt and caught Rome in the shoulder where it attempted to chew through his armor, but the tough scales kept the Garm from ripping into dragon flesh. Rome swung his head and knocked the Garm loose from its perch. The Garm flew across the meadow where it skidded to a stop.

The second Garm, still held tightly in the dragon's claw, raked wildly at Rome's wrist. Rome tried to unleash his eye fire on the squirming Garm, but only succeeded in lighting the grass by his foot on fire. Remembering his own warning to Julian, he quickly stomped it out with his massive, fire-resistant claws. This was the opportunity the Garm needed, and it took full advantage of it. The Garm twisted loose from the dragon's grip and ran swiftly away.

By the time the dragon was able to face his ex-captive again, the Garm had disappeared. Using his dragon sense, Rome knew that the Garm was using its stealth technique against him. He swung his head around to locate the other Garm, but it too had vanished.

"Be prepared, Jules," he warned his partner telepathically. "They have gone invisible on us."

Julian relocated to Rome's side. He used the dragon's huge body as a wall to prevent a rear attack. Using his enhanced vision, Rome surveyed the field hoping to catch a small movement or something to give away the Garms' position.

The object of this battle wasn't to kill the Garms. It was to simply drain enough of their energy to make them fade from the realm's existence. Both knight and dragon knew this challenge wasn't going to be easy. Every Garm attack drained precious energy but it also drained Rome and Julian as well. They had to attack and defend over and over again. They had to outlast and survive.

There weren't any clues suggesting the attacker's location. The dragon could feel his anger due to the loss of his prey begin to grow. It was a strange combination of stressful frustration and critical necessity. He swung his head from side to side in a distraught manner. This was getting him nowhere. Where were they?

"I will tear this entire glen apart until I find those monsters," Rome blustered. That is when he saw it. There were depressions in the grass off to his left moving in Julian's direction. The tiny blades of grass bent under the pressure of a Garm's weight. It was barely noticeable in the dim moonlight, but Rome could see it. He waited until his invisible aggressor was within striking distance.

"Duck!" roared Rome. Julian ducked behind Pridwen as Rome swung one of his claws just inches over his head.

A loud whacking noise sounded and Rome felt his backhanded strike made contact. Immediately the unconscious Garm became visible, flew ten feet in the air, and landed with a thud close to the tree line. Julian charged the motionless monster. He was upon the creature as it regained its composure. He performed a similar backhand attack with Pridwen knocking the creature upside its head and into the woods.

"To me, knight," roared Rome. Without thinking, Julian ran to his dragon who was struggling with the other invisible assailant. By the way the dragon was craning his neck and snapping his jaws, it looked like the undetectable Garm was attacking his back. Julian scampered up the dragon's tail adeptly avoiding his spikes, and lunged himself shield first to where he assumed the Garm was.

A concussive impact was made, and Julian crashed to the ground. Unfortunately, he lost possession of his breath AND Pridwen in the fall. The dragon felt for the unseen figure and upon finding it, seized the Garm with his sturdy claw. He picked it up and pummeled it into the ground, hoping to knock it unconscious. After three or four slams, the Garm became visible in between the dragon's talons.

Once Julian regained his mobility, he got to his feet, grabbed his shield, and attempted to aid in smashing the Garm's head. Without warning, the second Garm tackled Julian to the ground. When the two stopped rolling, Julian was able to position the shield between himself and the monster. The Garm stood over Julian with its face tentacles waving maniacally. It snapped its jaws at his face and scraped his shield with threatening claws. One furious swipe landed across Julian's helmet leaving a large scratch above the eyehole. Julian struggled with all his might to get the creature off of him, but it simply weighed too much. The Garm and knight battled furiously; neither getting the upper hand. Julian wondered how much longer the Garm could last. His energy must be depleting. He also knew that his energy was waning as well. As Julian reached limits of his physical ability, when instantaneously, the Garm flew off his chest.

"What the ...?" Julian thought.

"I am here," Rome replied. "Get to your feet and take yourself away until you are able to fight. I will handle these two miscreants."

Julian was too exhausted to argue. He got up and moved out of the dragon's way. It seemed strange that when Rome was in his true form as a dragon his personality changed. He became more aggressive and commanding. As the dragon took over, Rome seemed to lose some of his humanity. Not that Julian was complaining. There was nothing wrong with having a fire-breathing dragon as a partner. In fact, he couldn't think of any other kind of mythical animal he would rather be bonded to. Plus, he knew that when he was the knight, he also behaved differently. He was just worried about Rome. Julian promised himself that he would talk to both Rome and Mr. Jones about personality fluctuations if they made it out of this skirmish alive. Julian collapsed by the some bushes that crept into the glen safely hid from the Garms.

Meanwhile, back at the battle, Rome had wrapped his tail around the Garm's throat and lifted it off the ground. He whipped the beast back and forth trying to strangle the energy out of it, while still keeping a firm foothold on the other Garm that was thrashing violently to escape the dragon's clutches. The dragon held the two as long as he could, but at long last the one caught by Rome's tail got loose. Thinking that the knight was still incapacitated, Rome threw the Garm he held in his claw at the other one. He planned to eradicate both Garms with a full on collision. Two Garms, one stone.

As planned, the Garm struck the other one in mid-air and both were sent tumbling away from the dragon. They bounced along the ground and fell into a heap of limbs not far from the tree line. Rome did a double check to make sure both were clearly in his sight before he checked on his brother.

"Julian, are you alright?" Rome requested across the spatial linking.

"I'm fine, dude. Just a bit groggy," Julian sent to Rome sounding rather irritated. "Can we please torch these guys?" he asked Rome as he approached the dragon. Rome could see the scratches and abrasions Julian's armor had taken. This battle was significantly more onerous than the previous one. He glanced at the Garms as they collected themselves and nodded to his friend.

Julian pulled out his die and rolled it in the soft grass. Once Artemis materialized, he set up his ballistic attack. He could feel his energy drain. The use of magic cost Julian what little reserve power he had. He knew shooting the arrow and guiding it to its target could be more than he could bear, but it had to be done. He peaked up at his Dragon Master to analyze his symbiotic injuries. It was obvious that the continuous fighting was also taking its toll on Rome.

They wanted to end this now. Julian loosed a prized arrow which was aimed directly at one of the Garm's heads. Julian mustered a small battle cry. "For Camelot!"

Rome's chest swelled and glowed. Wearily, he blew fire and lit the arrow. Both dragon and knight watched the flaming missile arch through the air and struck true. Just like the last time, the Garm howled loudly and vanished.

"Good shootin' partner," breathed Julian, as he slowly succumbed to exhaustion.

Chapter Seventeen

Rome's was so weakened that his head spun. He blinked a few times trying to regain his focus. Since Julian had passed out, Rome was severely debilitated. Just another side effect of The Great Synergy. He had to pull from his reserve energy. He had to defeat the other Garm for his brother. He had to make sure it couldn't cause any havoc in his home town. Rome tried to flap his wings to set up a final barrage against the monster, but he was apparently too drained to fly. It looked like he would have to resort to fire breathing instead of physically dragon-handling his opponent.

"Think, think, think," Rome berated himself. "How can I beat this thing without causing any collateral damage?" Rome couldn't focus or use any of the dragon senses that he could usually call upon when in his true form. Is this what happens when he fights too hard? Why is he so out of shape? He was going to have to train harder.

Now, he needed to focus. He had a Garm to eradicate.

As if on cue, the Garm attacked. It came racing towards Rome with more vigor than seemed possible. Knowing it would take all he had left, Rome prepared his fire attack. He inhaled a huge breath of air, and his chest glowed like a furnace. It was obvious the Garm knew what was about to happen. Before Rome could launch an incendiary assault, the Garm hurled itself at Rome. Caught off guard, Rome's only option was to open his mouth and try to catch the Garm. Whether by luck or ability, Rome caught the Garm by one foot. The Garm shrieked and swiped fitfully at the dragon's face, with all its other extremities. Rome blocked and dodged to avoid the clawing beast.

"Enough," Rome thought. With renewed effort, Rome snaked his tail around the Garm's torso trapping it in the air. The Garm struggled to get out of the death grip, but its efforts were to no avail. Rome opened his mouth wide enough to inhale the flammable oxygen around his head. He turned to face the struggling Garm and blew a scorching blast of fire right at the Garm and up into the night sky. Its tentacles squirmed and it howled at Rome. A second later, the Garm disappeared from Earth's dimensional plane for eternity.

Relief flooded through Rome's body. It was over. Now all the dragon could think about was rest, food, and Julian. Julian! Where was Julian?

"I'm here, brother," replied the knight. Rome immediately turned in the direction of the voice. Julian was sitting propped up against a tree.

Rome trudged over to his brother. He collapsed beside Julian with such gravity that the ground shook. Smoke and steam escaped from his nostrils like a jalopy finally breaking down for the last time. In the deepest dragon voice he could summon Rome said, "I thought you said we could handle ten of those things?"

Julian leaned against his friend, the fire dragon who had just saved his skin and the town. "We can," he whispered. "And someday, we may have to." He laughed out loud. "Rome, from Volcana. Thank you for your bravery today. You are an exemplary warrior and a true blood brother."

Rome let out a small scoff. The boys had survived another attack by two very aggressive

Darkbrand hunters. Rome spoke up. "Sir Julian, we need to figure out better attack strategies for dealing with these things. Fending off two of them was exponentially harder than one. I cannot imagine how we would do it if we had an entire pack of them to incapacitate."

Julian rolled around to look at Rome in the eyes. "That's not even the worst part," he said. "Just wait until we run into a Minotaur or a couple of Nocturns." Julian swung his head back around and dropped his chin to his chest. "You are absolutely right. We have got to improve our fighting stratagems. The fire arrows work pretty well from long distance, but the hand-to-hand combat is a completely different ball game. Hopefully some of my other legendary weapons will be helpful when those scenarios present themselves!"

"Great, more paperclips!" teased Rome.

Julian jokingly punched at the dragon's shoulder. "Yeah," he teased. "And if they don't work, we can always open an office supply company."

It was great to have Julian there to add lightness and levity to an otherwise bleak situation.

Knight and dragon relaxed. Rome felt pleased with himself and rated himself as having done a fair job. Sure, luck had played a great part in the victory, but it is often better to be lucky than good.

Then Rome heard it. Something was moving in the woods. He snaked his head around to look into the menacing woods. Someone was there. He couldn't see them, but he knew they were there; WATCHING. The dragon moved quickly. He ran towards where he could hear the light falling of footsteps and complex breathing. That's when he saw a figure rapidly moving deeper into the woods.

Rome chased after the mystery figure. He dodged between trees trying to gain on the shadow, but his bulk impeded his progress. He needed to fly! He tried to flap his wings, but he was still too exhausted to leave the ground. There was no way a dragon could possibly keep up with the watcher who seemed to be gliding above the ground. The shadow darted around trees and through thick brush while making very little noise. Rome tried his best to follow the same path. Eventually, he smacked into a young pine, and his wing got caught in some of the branches. He struggled to free himself, never once taking his eyes off the hooded figure. He finally broke free by simply trampling over the tree that imprisoned him. He could still see the figure, but it was putting a lot of distance between them.

Rome continued to follow, losing ground with each passing second. He veered around another set of trees and abruptly stopped in his tracks to avoid colliding with a different figure. To avoid the collision, Rome flung his body to the left and rolled into a pile of wooden debris.

"Oh, great Colossus!" shrieked Mr. Jones who immediately covered his face and shrunk into the fetal position on the ground.

Quickly, for a large dragon, Rome got to his paws. Ignoring Mr. Jones, he looked around for the shadow figure, but it was gone. Brushing pine needles and dirt off of his white shirt, Mr. Jones cautiously approached the dragon. He readjusted his glasses and tried to get the dragon's attention without being to abrupt. Before he could say anything, Rome turned to face the older man. The look on the dragon's face gave Mr. Jones quite a start.

"Mr. Jones," Rome said in and anxious voice that matched his expression. "Did you see that shadow running through the woods? I was following it, but I could not keep up."

"No, Rome," said Mr. Jones obviously shaken. "I saw no such thing. I only saw a four thousand-pound dragon coming right at me. I thought for sure I would be flattened."

"There is someone out there in the woods, magician," said Rome pivoting his head from side to side. "They were watching the knight and me. I chased them, but they were too agile and too fast."

There was a flash, and Rome was converted back into his human form. He looked over his shoulder and saw his brother running up to them. Julian placed his hands on his knees and hung his head panting in short gasps.

"Dude!" he labored. "Why did you take off like that? Never leave your brother behind!" He sat down on the ground breathing sharply. He rolled the die in his hands. "How am I supposed to back you up, man?"

"You are right, Jules," Rome acquiesced. "I am really sorry for running off, but I saw something or someone moving in the woods. They were watching us. They were really fast too. I mean, it was like they were flying across the ground. Hovering, you know? Who could it be? Why would someone want to watch us battle those creepy monsters?" Rome threw his hands in the air in obvious frustration. "Just what we need, another individual who knows our secret."

Julian looked up from his seat. "Maybe we have a super fan?"

Mr. Jones piped up. "Young Master, there are still many things we don't know about the upcoming battles. There may be players involved that are obscured to us right now as well. Perhaps we should reconvene to your school and do some brainstorming. While we are there, we should also check to make sure the sealing spell worked. I would like to take some time to think about who would find an interest in our activities."

It was a long walk back to the school. Mr. Jones would not let the boys transform again, just in case the shadow was still around. They had changed into knight and dragon at school before the shadow was watching. They had changed back after the shadow was gone. Mr. Jones wanted very much to keep the boys identity a secret as long as possible. He didn't want to jeopardize the mission by making the boys media darlings just yet.

Julian recalled how bravely he had fought in the battle on the way back. Rome laughed to himself at how animated Julian was in his description to Mr. Jones. He even relived the highlights of the battle using Mr. Jones as a tackling dummy. Mr. Jones was amazed that they had successfully defended the realm twice now and defeated three Garms in total. That was three more of the Darkbrand army that would need to wait hundreds if not thousands of years before they could attempt another breach from The Void.

Mr. Jones and Julian spent several minutes discussing the other beings that existed in The Void. Questions arose and were answered about fighting strategies and Julian's magic weapons. Rome walked in silence. Mr. Jones made the point that there were still worse things in The Void which had not reared their ugly heads yet. He reiterated that they would have to improve their training significantly if anything more evil showed up around town. Hopefully, the sealing spell had worked at the school so they could cross that portal off their list of invasion spots.

Upon arriving at the school cafeteria, Julian found the door locked. Confused, Julian said, "It was open the last time we came here. I wonder if the police got called, and Officer Benton came to lock it up." He struggled comically with the door trying to open it.

Mr. Jones snickered and pushed his glasses back onto his nose. "The door has been locked EVERY time," he said. "What kind of school leaves its backdoors open at all hours of the night? I have been allowing you safe passage into the school with one of my spells. It's called transportation incantation." Mr. Jones bowed his head and extended one arm out to the side. "It creates a seamless passageway between two points. I have merely been focusing it on you two and the interior of the school. To you, it appears as though you have been walking right in, but my spell is the only way you would have access." Mr. Jones raised one finger at the boys. "To prevent someone from abusing this by performing atrocities such as walking into a bank, it has been limited to the hands of those who would use it only for good. Imagine what could transpire if evil got ahold of it." Mr. Jones touched his chin with his fore fingers. "I can do even more powerful things with it as well. For instance, I could instantly transport a small group of people somewhere else in the world for a limited amount of time." He clapped his hands together. "But for my next trick, allow me to get us inside this school."

Mr. Jones removed his glasses and closed his eyes. He began murmuring strange words to himself and bobbing his head slightly. As he continued the whispering chant, there was a blue flash of light around the perimeter of the door. It rumbled faintly and then stood still.

Mr. Jones stopped his humming and motioned for Rome to open the door. Rome followed his lead and reached for the handle to pull it open. However, this time he noticed that the door flickered a little. He also noticed that the handle appeared to be briefly pixelated like everything else that he had come across lately. Rome thought to himself that the pixelating must be tied to everything magical. He wondered what else he had never noticed in his daily life that may be tainted by magic. He would start taking notice now.

Chapter Eighteen

Once inside the school, the trio made for the water fountain/portal just outside the library. Rome found it funny that both portals here in Georgia were located near libraries. Another thing he needed to talk to Mr. Jones about. He better start making a list. As a boy, his memory wasn't the best, and as a dragon, none of these questions seemed to matter.

Mr. Jones stayed behind the boys a few paces just in case he would need protection. He was really only there to look into the portal with his glasses and make sure it was sealed. The boys determined that his magic did not extend to battling barbarities from The Void.

As they neared the fountain, Rome listened and sensed that all was clear. Mr. Jones excused himself and pushed past the boys. He dropped to his knees, and thoroughly inspected all the parameters of the water fountain. Before he got up to deliver the good news, he noticed something on the floor directly under the portal. It was about three inches long, circular, and bonelike. It closely resembled a smooth skeletal cone or the tip of an ivory horn. What could that be doing here? With a sudden realization of the truth, he rose. Hiding the horn in one of the pockets of his coat, he delivered the good news to his students.

"By the Kraken's tentacles, you've done it, boys!" he exclaimed. "I see no signs of reemergence emanating from this portal. It appears that Mr. Rider's knowledge and supplies have indeed closed this hellish thing for good. I can see many of them in there squirming around on top of each other." He pulled off his glasses and began chewing on them. "But they will find no sanction at this interchange."

The boys were elated. Rome and Julian exchanged multiple high fives, but Mr. Jones seemed somewhat reserved for such a celebration. Both boys noticed Mr. Jones's limited pleasure about the portal and exchanged apprehensive frowns.

"What's wrong with Mr. Jones?" Julian thought across the spatial linking. "You would think that he would be dancing a jig about this whole thing. I don't get it."

"Me neither," Rome thought back. "Should we ask him? I bow to your expertise in matters of human emotions since I am only a dense, brutish dragon."

Both boys chuckled, causing Mr. Jones to look at them dubiously.

"What is so humorous?" asked Mr. Jones in a somewhat taxing tone. "This whole situation is one of the utmost seriousness. Just because you defeated a few Garms does not mean we are out of the woods yet." Mr. Jones paused and chuckled at his opportune pun. "Well, you know what I mean." He got serious again. "You both need to train persistently so you can protect yourselves and each other. I will not have anything happening to you. You are just boys after all."

"Whoa. Mr. Jones, where did that come from?" said Julian in deep concern. "You said yourself that the portal was closed, and we sent three Garms back to The Void for a very long time. What has gotten you in such a state?"

Slowly, Mr. Jones pulled the fractured horn from his jacket pocket. He held it up so the boys could see. Julian took it from the old man's hand and inspected the object cautiously. He noticed that the bottom on the object was perfectly planed as if it had been sliced by a laser. Julian handed the fragment to Rome who immediately smelled it and pulled away in disgust.

"What is this?" Rome demanded. "It smells of pure evil. Where did you find it?"

"It was under the drinking fountain," admitted Mr. Jones. "I believe that something much stronger and more malicious than a Garm was about to come forth when the sealing spell closed the portal. Only the tip of the foul beast's horn bridged our world. If this is true, we are closer to catastrophic events than I previously believed. In my opinion, this is the tip of a Minotaur's horn." Mr. Jones paused for dramatic effect. "That means all manner of beasts from The Void have stored enough energy to cross over into our world. We need to learn much, much more, not only about our roles in the fight, but also about the enemies we are certain to encounter. We need to search out allies, as I am convinced we cannot win this war alone. We need to find ways to strengthen your bonds with each other. And lastly, I am not sure that I am wise enough or strong enough to guide you to victory"

Both boys tried to speak at once. Julian, in his inevitable way won the battle. Looking at Rome for support, Julian would speak for the pair. Suddenly, the boys felt a deep link connect between them. This was right. This was how it was supposed to be. The knight speaks for the pair. The dragon backs up the knights words. There would always be discussions and compromises, but in the end both would do their part. Rome looked at Julian. Julian nodded. Without thinking they both knew.

"Mr. Jones," Julian began. "We know there is tons more to learn. And you are right about us needing allies. But please don't sell YOURSELF short. Without you, Rome and I would never have found each other. You helped us perform The Great Synergy and complete Rome's heart. If given a choice between the true Merlin and you for our guide, we would both chose you. You know us. We know you. That is all that matters." Julian placed a hand on Mr. Jones's shoulder. "I'm not sure how, but we will find everything we need to defeat the creatures of The Void. This is our world and we will protect it with your help!"

Mr. Jones looked affectionately at the boys. He appreciated their trust and love. Maybe they could figure it out together. But how? Mr. Jones nodded and made a motion with his hand for the group to head home. After all, they were trespassing.

They turned together and began to walk towards the open exit. As they started to enter the cafeteria, something caught Rome's eye. It wasn't a shadowy figure or an evil monster from The Void. It was a bright orange flyer posted on the cafeteria window. Something drew him to it; something like that same peculiar feeling he had in Mrs. Case's office.

The flyer read

Are You Ready For Some EXCITEMENT?

Make your classes extra special this year by joining us.

Study abroad in The United Kingdom!

Ask your homeroom teacher for an application

Visit London, Oxford, Stonehenge and many other landmark attractions
4 weeks this Spring!

Prices are not yet determined

Must have parental consent

Rome pulled the flyer off the wall. "Hey," he said, "Now this would be awesome! I bet we could find all the information we ever needed there. After all is not England where the original good versus evil war thing took place?" Rome started to get excited. "Jules, you could go and do all the research that needs to be done. And Mr. Jones, you could transport yourself over there to keep Jules on track." Rome laughed to himself a little. "He gets distracted pretty easily." Rome suddenly had a saddening thought. "I would love to go, but there is NO WAY my folks could afford to send me to Europe for a semester."

"Well," Julian chimed in. "Mine can. And they can pay for you too, Rome. I'll tell my dad it has to do with my training, and that I am priming you to be my squire. He will totally go for it."

"It helps to have friends in high places," said Mr. Jones. "Julian, find out what you can about this endeavor, and perhaps we will begin a new adventure. However, I'm not sure I will be able to join you on this portion of the quest to save our realm. I am relegated to my watchful duties here. I have faith in you boys, though. Let us undertake this with the hopes of finding answers to our questions and solutions to our quest."

Mr. Jones took the boys out for pizza and ice cream. The boys had not eaten in some time and were famished. Besides sating their physical needs, it gave them time to talk over the possibilities of a trip to England. Mr. Jones knew that the peace they had obtained would not stay for very long. Eventually, the Darkbrands would find a new hole to crawl through in their never-ending attempt to retake the land they once ruled. They always did. However, he was very enthusiastic about the team he had put together. It took eight years to get to this point, and though there were still many questions to answer, he felt positive that they would make a serious difference in the world.

Mr. Jones let his mind wander about other pressing matters. What of the others? Mr. Jones knew there were other players contributing in their own ways to the battle for Earth. In fact, he knew very much about one of them. What if there were others fighting the same battles behind clandestine fronts? Perhaps getting to England, where The Despot War eventuated, was exactly what they needed. They would be without him, but he had confidence in his two young warriors. They had made him proud thus far.

The boys left the pizzeria and went their separate ways for the evening. Rome was thrilled about possibly taking a trip across the pond to Merry 'Ole England. It was a distant land with a long, secretive history. He was sure they would find more on how to prevent the invasion if only they could get Mr. Rider to pay for their trip. Rome did not like the idea of groveling to Mr. Rider to become the benefactor. It almost made him sick to think they needed his money and permission to continue their activities. Why did Rome feel such disgust towards Mr. Rider? Was it just the name thing?

Rome was so deep in his own thoughts that he didn't see the same mysterious figure from before watching him from upon a wall. It followed him for five or six blocks before darting down a black alleyway. It watched him turn into his neighborhood and take a right onto his street. Something around the neck of the shadow started glowing faintly. It eventually turned into a glaring red orb that seemed to be attached to a necklace. It was definitely watching Rome.

Suddenly, a chill shot up Rome's back and his sense went off like fireworks. The shadow had become complacent as Rome walked deep in thought. Now, it was caught in plain sight. Rome sent a warning to Julian about the shadow as he turned to face it. Without his dragon vision, Rome could only make out a few details about the figure. He was pretty sure it was a woman. He wasn't sure if it was a human woman though as the light from the orb distorted its face.

"You there," he shouted at the figure. "What do you want? You have been following me all night." He pulled out his cell phone and said, "I am calling the police right now!"

The woman turned and once again began to drift away at superhuman speed.

"That's right, you better glide out of here! I'm not afraid of you! You have been warned," Rome said with some bravado.

As the figure disappeared, Rome started back towards his destination. He debated following the figure, but chose to run home instead. The strange light hanging from its neck gave Rome a grander sense of dread than he had gotten in his dragon form. This cryptic person seemed troubling to Rome and probably dangerous. He was glad to see her flee.

What a night Rome thought feeling a little unnerved. Garms, a mysterious woman, a deep special linking to his blood brother, and tons of pizza; who could ask for more. Sleep, yes sleep was what he needed right now.

Chapter Nineteen

The next day, Julian found Rome in the halls by the water fountain. Rome looked like he had healed up nicely after a long sleep. Julian, on the other hand, looked like he had stayed up all night recounting the events of the previous evening over and over. It was just another example of the boy's differing personalities. Both boys eyed the fountain cautiously as they struck up an excited conversation.

"Rome, dude!" said Julian eagerly. "My dad said he would pay for BOTH of us to go study abroad this spring." Julian changed his voice to an over-exaggerated British accent. "We get to go to England and rub elbows with the Brits! Fish and chips! Big Ben an' all that lot!"

The same girl who stared them down the other day walked by with a hand full of books. She stopped, looked at Julian, and shook her head before moving on down the hall.

"Great, Jules," explained Rome. "But did you get my warning about the mysterious woman last night? I caught a decent look at her. She was wearing a hooded cloak and some type of glowing necklace. There was something very familiar about her, but I cannot quite put my claw on it."

"Man, I thought you were kidding," said Julian tilting his head. "I seriously thought you were just testing out our new and improved connection." Suddenly, Julian's eyes got wide and he sputtered out questions at a rapid pace. "You mean there really was someone there? Did you get anything from your dragon senses? Did you call the police? Did you try to take her on yourself? How do you know it was a woman? Was she pretty?"

Rome groaned to himself. "Knock it off, Jules! There WAS actually a person there. At least, I think she was a person. She was stalking me on my way home from Pizza Zone. I am fairly confident it was the same figure that watched us in the woods after the Garm battle."

Julian stared at Rome. "Are...are you sure, man?" he asked doubtfully. "You know, I never even saw anyone last night in the woods. Neither did Mr. Jones. Maybe you got knocked too hard in the head or something." Julian crossed his eyes and stuck out his tongue.

"Hey!" flared Rome. "I am not seeing things or concussed. She was there. She was following me. I think I saw her smiling. It was pretty creepy." Rome paused. "Anyway, what kind of backup are you if you are going to be constantly ignoring my messages? I have to be able to rely on you, Jules!"

"Yeah, sorry, dude," lamented Julian. "Honestly, I was in a bind. I had a nail biter of epic proportions going into the fourth quarter of a game of Tecmo Bowl. You know how I get with those video games, man. I guess I kinda neglected the responsibility." He shrugged and smiled wryly. "But it won't happen again, dude. Scout's honor."

"You are hardly a scout," frowned Rome.

"And you don't have beautiful, mysterious women following you around everywhere," joked Julian. He tossed his die in the air and caught it right before it hit the ground. He brought it up to eye level so Rome could see the one pip. "Not yet, anyways!"

"Ok, never mind about the woman," he said. "Can we talk about our trip to England? We have to remember that the main reason we are going is to find out as much as we can about The Tyrant King and his minions. That is our main goal." Rome paused because Julian had suddenly turned sour. "Why the long face?" Rome tested.

"Well, there is ONE condition of our trip," said Julian. "My dad said he would pay for us to go, but we have to spend some of our free time with my little sister." Julian cradled his head in his hands like an overzealous stage actor for this next part. "I don't know if I told you, but she is in a boarding school in England. It is sort of a family tradition. Young boys stay with the family to learn all about being a knight, and the girls go to a particular finishing school in Somerset to learn how to be a Lady. She's only nineteen months younger than me, but we are completely different people. She's very nosy and picks up on anything you don't want her to know. That means we have to be super secretive about our real agenda. We can't let her know about The Great Synergy. She'll totally narc me out to my dad. And if that happens, not only will we be yanked back to Georgia, but also I'm grounded for life."

"No problem," soothed Rome. "We can just make her show us around town and do our homework. She is smart, right?" This gave Rome a frightening thought. Could Julian's sister be WORSE than him? Was that even possible?

A fly began to buzz around Julian's head. He swatted wildly at it. "Yeah," he said. "She's smart. Maybe too smart. I don't want her finding out about our alliance." He ducked his head and swung his arm trying hit the fly. "Besides, Mr. Jones won't be with us either. It's gonna be only you and me!" The fly landed on Julian's head. He smacked at it several times to get it out of his hair. "Dang lunchroom lettin' all the flies in!" he exclaimed. "And that brings me to some more bad news. The county has to send chaperones with us from the school. I asked my dad if he would volunteer, but apparently it has to be all faculty. So, guess who's going with us?"

As if she had heard the entire conversation and was entering on cue, Mrs. Case came around the corner and approached the boys. Her soft blue eyes seemed to hypnotize them as she spoke. "Mr. Lockheed and Mr. Rider. I understand you two will be accompanying me and the others on our trip to England? I heard from your father last night,

Julian. He is an extraordinary man. He thought it was an excellent idea. In fact, he said it would be "an awe-inspiring adventure of the mind". I simply love it when parents take a positive interest in our scholarly functions." She put her fingers to her lips and giggled a little. "I look forward to sharing this once in a lifetime experience with you boys. The world is such a big place. It will do us all some good to explore the entirety of the realm. Who knows what secrets are out there? Who knows what will be discovered?" She paused for a brief second. "Julian, lad, there's a fly on your head."

She walked away as Julian furiously swatted at himself trying to kill the fly. After a few seconds he stopped and waited for the fly to land again. It touched down on Rome's shoulder and buzzed its wings a few times. Rome turned his head carefully and winked some of his eye fire at the insect sending it flying down the hall to bother someone else.

"There is just something about that lady that does not set right with me," Rome whispered. "Did you notice how she used the word "realm"? Spooky, huh?" Rome shook off any ideas about Mrs. Case and focused back on the task at hand. "But, you are right, Jules. This is going to be our hardest task yet. Without Mr. Jones, we are going to be on our own."

Julian looked around for the fly then stared at Rome. "Thanks," he said somewhat sarcastically. He launched his book bag onto his back and headed down the hallway, but then turned suddenly. "By the way, Cecilia Parker is also on the list of kids going to England. You'll be spending lots of time with her in a foreign land, and with limited adult supervision. You going to show her how cool you are? I can't wait to watch that train wreck." Julian threw his head back and belted out some exaggerated laughter on his way to class.

Rome snickered to himself then turned to take a sip of water from the fountain. He pressed down on the button, but before drinking any of the water, he checked the foreign- looking inscription one last time. It did not shimmer. It did not radiate. It was still and quiet.

Rome smiled and brought the cool liquid to his lips. He looked forward to more adventures with his blood brother. His world had been flipped upside down in just a couple of weeks. Who knew his original act of defiance would ultimately lead him to where he was now? More or less, he'd been thrust into the role of an undercover dragon and charged with defending the Earth from a gathering of fiends frothing at the mouth to barge through inter-planetary portals. Even funnier were the characters posed to be his partners in this chore. For as far as Rome could see into the future, he would be accompanied by a whimsical, librarian with a penchant for observing alternate dimensions and an audacious, brash, magical knight with conformity and censorship issues. It was quite a change from how things used to be. The days used to really drag on where he lived, but he would soon find out how unbelievably exciting those days could be.

The End

(or is it just the beginning?)

Made in the USA
Monee, IL
19 October 2022